VANISHING POINT

Other Claire Reynier Mysteries
by Judith Van Gieson

The Stolen Blue

VANISHING
POINT

A Claire Reynier Mystery

JUDITH VAN GIESON

University of New Mexico Press
Albuquerque

Library of Congress Cataloging-in-Publication Data

Van Gieson, Judith, 1941–
    Vanishing Point : a Claire Reynier mystery / Judith Van Gieson.
— 1st ed.
        p.   cm.
    ISBN 0-8263-2383-9 (alk. paper)
    1. Women archivists—Fiction. 2. Missing persons—Fiction.
3. New Mexico—Fiction. 4. Authors—Fiction. I. Title.
    PS3572.A42224   V36   2001
    811' .54—dc21   00-011153

✳

Vanishing Point is dedicated to my former roommate
and longtime friend, Danielle Freeman,
and to the world's best fans,
Katia Kirpane and Gerard Kosicki, with thanks
for sharing the wonder and the journey.

HUNDREDS OF TIMES I HAVE TRUSTED MY LIFE TO CRUMBLING SANDSTONE AND NEARLY VERTICAL ANGLES IN THE SEARCH FOR WATER OR CLIFF DWELLINGS . . . ONE WAY AND ANOTHER, I HAVE BEEN FLIRTING PRETTY HEAVILY WITH DEATH, THE OLD CLOWN.

—Everett Ruess

1

Chapter One

Archivists are known as the keepers of memory. One of Claire Reynier's jobs at the Center for Southwest Research at the University of New Mexico was to preserve the papers, the legend, and the memory of the writer Jonathan Vail. There was little in his own words—a few letters, a novel, and a journal that had remained in print for more than thirty years—but volumes had been written about him. Claire liked to think of Jonathan as the literary West's phantom limb. In 1966, when he was twenty-three, he vanished on a camping trip in Slickrock Canyon in southeastern Utah. The journal he was keeping at the time was never found. But, as a brain continues to receive signals from a limb it knows has been severed, people who cared about Western writing continued to receive stimuli from Jonathan Vail. For years after he vanished there were sightings all over the West, in Mexico, and in Canada. His initials were found carved in caves and on canyon walls.

Southeastern Utah is a good place to start a legend: the mesas are vast, the canyons are deep and often invisible until a person stands right on the edge, the rocks are whipped into suggestive shapes by the water and the wind. When Jonathan disappeared, he was young, good-looking, and full of promise, and that was how he remained. Claire knew well enough that while real people show the effects of time, legends don't. She had once been five years younger than Jonathan, but that was long ago. She had recently turned fifty-one. He would always be twenty-three. Eventually she would die and be remembered by friends and family, but the legend of Jonathan Vail would last as long as people cared to read about the West.

Claire had a layperson's knowledge of Jonathan Vail's work when she came to the center and was put in charge of his papers. She had been a student at the University of Arizona during the years he dropped in and out of UNM. She knew of him—everyone did—but they had never met. She read his novel, *A Blue-Eyed Boy*, when she was eighteen and was enthralled by Jonathan's brand of rebellion and his elegant and passionate prose style.

The Vail family had donated the original manuscripts of the journal and *A Blue-Eyed Boy* to the center with the stipulation that they could be read only by scholars. If a scholar wanted to read them, Claire retrieved the manuscripts from their place in the tower and took them to the Anderson Reading Room, where valuable manuscripts were read. Scholars were required to surrender their ID's and put on the white gloves provided by library staff before they were allowed to touch precious pages. After Claire had read *A Blue-Eyed Boy* several times and discussed it innumerable times, she'd come to the conclusion that it was a book best read when one was eighteen. The coming-of-age theme would always be of interest, and Vail showed a poet's flair in his descriptions of the natural world, but attitudes that had once seemed bold and flamboyant now verged on self-indulgence. Nevertheless, Claire didn't consider it her job to disillusion a student captivated by the book or the legend, and by now the legend had become greater than the book. The possibility still existed that the mystery of Vail's disappearance would be solved, and Claire listened patiently to all the theories.

The night Jonathan vanished from Slickrock Canyon, he was with his girlfriend, Jennie Dell. Her story, which had remained constant, was that they went to sleep in a cave during a light rain. When she woke up, she was alone, the rain had become a downpour, and the water level was rising rapidly in the narrow canyon. Jennie claimed that it was hours before the water receded sufficiently for her to go looking for Jonathan. By then any footprints or evidence had washed away.

Jonathan was reckless enough (possibly even drugged enough) to have wandered off alone. Slickrock got its name because it turned treacherously slippery when wet. He might have slipped, fallen off a cliff, drowned in the flash flood. He could have been struck by lightning or a rattlesnake. The accidental death theory was popular, but it had never satisfied Claire; she thought that sooner or later Jonathan's bones would have been found. Bones don't lie, and they take forever to disintegrate. Occasionally human bones *were* found downstream from Slickrock Canyon, but DNA testing established that they were not Jonathan Vail's.

He had received his draft notice shortly before he vanished, and some people believed he killed himself in despair or staged his own disappearance to avoid the Vietnam War. Rumors persisted that Jonathan had fathered a child and that he was alive and well somewhere. None of these theories satisfied Claire either. If there had been a suicide, there should have been a body. When he disappeared, Jonathan was a young, acclaimed writer, full of books yet to be written. Claire believed that a writer of Vail's reputation would not have killed himself. She was sure he would have returned when amnesty was granted and continued writing. In her experience writers lived to write. If something had happened to Jonathan in exile, word would have come back.

She thought the most logical explanation for his disappearance was that he had been murdered and the remains buried deep or carted away. Jennie Dell, while never charged with a crime, was still shadowed by suspicion. But the theories Claire heard most often from graduate students had to do with cattle rustlers, drug dealers, Navajo thieves, a rancher who came upon Vail killing his cattle. The fact that the crime was never solved was blamed on the inexperience, incompetence, or indifference of Curt Devereux, the ranger who had conducted the investigation.

Long before Claire took charge of Vail's papers the sightings had stopped, and the initials that were still occasionally discovered carved in the walls of remote canyons were attributed to vandals from another era. The number of people who hoped to make their mark by solving the mystery or finding the journal that Jonathan was working on had dwindled to a handful of graduate students at UNM.

When Tim Sansevera, a doctoral candidate in American Studies, showed up in her office, Claire's first reaction was skepticism. Tim's scruffy appearance didn't help. Claire didn't expect anyone with a theory about Jonathan Vail to show up in a three-piece suit, but it wouldn't have hurt Tim's credibility any to have showered and changed his clothes. Although his surname was

Spanish, his appearance was Anglo: fair, sunburned skin, pale green eyes, and long reddish-brown hair pulled back in a ponytail. Tim wore a dirty T-shirt, torn jeans, and running shoes that had been tinted pink by dust. The hair on his forehead was matted with sweat.

He dropped his backpack to the floor and sat down in the chair across from Claire's desk. "I've been in Slickrock Canyon for a week," he said. Claire was willing to believe him on that score; he had the rank smell of a person who'd spent a week on the trail. She also knew that a discovery was a discovery wherever you found it. In the Southwest, discoveries were more likely to be made in the dust than anywhere else. "I drove straight here. I didn't even go home first."

Claire was feeling a tingle of excitement in spite of herself. "What did you find?"

"I was in the side canyon they call Sin Nombre, walking along a high ledge just below the mesa. It's a hard ledge to follow because it's full of rock slides. I'd been there before, but it seemed like the slides had shifted since the last trip. There might have been a hard rain, maybe even a minor earthquake. Anyway, I was able to climb over the rubble, which I never could before. I saw an opening. I climbed in." With an actor's sense of timing, Tim paused to retie his bandanna.

Claire distrusted his theatricality. What could he have seen? Another set of initials carved in the wall of a cave, that might have been opened and closed by rock slides numerous times in the last thirty years?

"I found this," he said, bending over and opening his backpack. "I brought it to you because the center is where it belongs." Tim took his find out of the backpack and handed it to her. It was a briefcase made of a thick gray hide and layered with dust.

"Did you open it?" Claire asked.

Tim nodded, focusing his intense green eyes on her.

"What did you find?"

"The journal," he whispered.

The *journal* could only be Jonathan Vail's journal. His last known words. The document that people had been searching the canyonlands for since 1966. The document that just might solve the mystery of his disappearance. Given the remoteness, ruggedness and dryness of the area in which he had vanished, it was entirely possible that the journal had sat in a cave undiscovered and well preserved for more than thirty years.

"Did you read it?" Claire asked, trying to resist the temptation to get theatrical herself.

"I didn't want to get fingerprints on it or damage it in any way. I read the first and last pages only."

That's what she would have done. Better not to have read the manuscript or even touched it, but for anyone familiar with the Vail legend it would have been hard to resist reading the first page to see if the handwriting was Vail's and the last page to see if the mystery had been solved.

"It's his," Tim said, radiating excitement like a canyon wall emanates heat. "It's his writing. It's his style."

Possible, Claire thought, but it wouldn't be the first elaborate hoax perpetrated in New Mexico. She had no reason to distrust Tim, though. As far as she knew, he was a dedicated student. He'd asked to read the manuscript of *A Blue-Eyed Boy* several times, but that wasn't unusual for someone doing a dissertation on the author. Maybe he was radiating too much heat—or was it that the stakes were too high? Claire reached into her desk drawer and pulled out a pair of white gloves. Tim watched as she inserted her hands, smoothing her fingers into place. It was a ritual she enjoyed, a way of showing reverence for something rare and valuable. The contrast between the pristine white gloves and the dusty gray briefcase was extreme.

She undid the zipper carefully, trying not to dirty the gloves, and slid her hand inside, feeling that there was an empty pocket in the side of the briefcase and that the leather was thick.

"What kind of hide is this?" she asked Tim. "Buffalo?"

"I don't know," he replied.

Claire pulled out a faded blue spiral-bound notebook and carefully turned back the cover. The paper was dry and crinkly, apparently with age. The ink was faded but still legible, the handwriting familiar. It was either Jonathan Vail's careless script, which Claire knew well, or a skillful forgery. The immensity of the discovery began to overwhelm her, and she closed her eyes. In her world this was comparable to finding a previously unknown Emily Dickinson poem or a sonnet by Shakespeare.

"Incredible, isn't it?" Tim asked.

"Yes."

She read the first entry, which was dated June 29, 1966. "Pale blue ribbon cloud sky. A hawk flew over the rim dangling a snake from its talons. A rare day when you get to see a *snake* and a *hawk*." It was Jonathan's handwriting. Jonathan's elliptical style.

Claire turned the pages carefully until she came to the last entry. Here the handwriting was larger, bolder, and even more careless than it had been at the beginning. The last entry was dated July 12, 1966, two days before Jennie Dell reported Jonathan missing. "Canyon slipping and sliding like the walls of La Sagrada Familia. Thunder growls in the distance like an angry bear or a drum roll. I hate the fucking war."

For an instant the sounds, the smells, the excitement of being young in 1966 came back to Claire. It was a time of living dangerously and Jonathan Vail could take her back there if anyone could. She was eager to read the rest of the journal, but there was much to be done first.

"Have you ever been to La Sagrada Familia?" she asked Tim.

"Never. Where is it?"

"It's an unfinished church in Barcelona designed by the architect Antonio Gaudí. The walls give the effect of sliding off the frame." Claire thought she knew as much about Jonathan as anyone, but she had never heard of him visiting Spain.

"I thought he was referring to the rain and rock slides in the canyon."

As Claire recalled, it hadn't started raining hard until July 13, a detail that was certain to be checked later when the manuscript was examined by scholars She would have to make one very careful copy, placing each page of the notebook on the Xerox machine's glass, and then recopy the copy so it could be read by the family and members of the department.

"Were you alone when you found this?" she asked Tim.

"Yes."

"Have you told anyone else?"

"Not yet."

"Was there anything else in the cave?" she asked. Footprints, tools, bones, murder weapons? she thought.

"Just a duffel bag."

"Did you look inside?"

"There were clothes on top, but I didn't go through it. I didn't want to disturb anything. The bag was heavy and I was carrying too much gear to bring it out."

"There are people who will say you should have left the briefcase there, too."

In its own way it was an archaeological find, although not ancient enough to be governed by the Antiquities Act. The thinking now was that archaeological finds should be left undisturbed.

"I know," Tim sighed, "but I couldn't. Someone who didn't value the journal might have found it. Suppose there was another slide? It might have gotten lost forever."

"Jonathan's disappearance is a cold case, but it's an unsolved case. The federal government could consider the journal evidence and moving it tampering with evidence. You would only have had to leave it alone long enough to get to the ranger station."

"I didn't want to report it to the ranger station. They fucked it up the first time, didn't they?" Claire felt the heat rising as his face flushed. It was beginning to seem fitting to her that Tim had found the journal; he had the same pale eyes and passionate intensity that his hero was known for.

"Who knows? We weren't there. We don't know the obstacles the rangers were facing."

"I'd hate to see them pawing all over the journal."

"I'm sure they can work with a copy. I do need to notify the rangers in Grand Gulch that you found the journal. They'll want to get in touch with you."

Tim wrote his address down on a slip of paper and handed it to Claire. "Before you call them, put the original in a very safe place."

"Of course. I'll also need to notify the family."

"*Them?* What did they ever do for Jonathan when he was alive?"

Jonathan's troubled relationship with authority was well documented in *A Blue-Eyed Boy*. He was drafted at age twenty-three, a few years from the outer limit of eligibility, by a hard-nosed draft board. It was widely believed that he could have avoided the draft by going to work for the family business, which manufactured felt that the army used, but Jonathan either refused to work for his family or the family refused to hire him. Claire had heard both theories.

"Legally the journal belongs to the heirs, who presumably are the parents. They have been very generous with the library. I have to ask their permission before we can do anything."

"Then what?"

"Hopefully, they'll allow us to keep the journal at the center and make it available to scholars, as they have the other papers."

"The journal is a major find. It should be published and read by everyone," Tim said.

He'd had five hours to think about this while driving down from Utah. Claire had had only a few minutes, and she hadn't even considered publication yet. "Well, of course, publication would be an option if the family is willing. UNM Press would be the logical choice."

"Not them!" Tim cried. "The journal should reach a wider audience."

"I don't know, Tim. It's been more than thirty years since Jonathan Vail disappeared. The journal is news here, but not everywhere."

Tim tugged at his bandanna. "It would be fair if my name appeared on the book, since I was the one who found the manuscript."

They were both in a publish-or-perish profession. If Tim intended to be an academic, having his name on such a prestigious publication when he was so young would jump-start his career. It would also be a coup for Claire, who was considered a member of the faculty and, as such, was required to publish. "It is a possibility, but it's premature to talk about publication. As I said, there are other things that need to be taken care of first."

Claire stood up. "Thank you so much for bringing this to me, Tim. It will be wonderful for the center."

"This is where it belongs," Tim said. "Will you call me when the copies are ready? I want to read all of it."

"Of course."

After Tim left, she slid the notebook back into the briefcase and balanced the package in her white gloved hands, reveling in the center's good fortune. Claire had been a librarian for twenty-five years and had never held a document she valued so much. She wanted to read it, authenticate it, solve the mystery of Jonathan Vail's disappearance. But first she had to copy the journal and report the discovery to Harrison Hough, the director of the center.

She took the journal to the Xerox machine, placed each page carefully on the glass, and made a copy. Then she copied the copy. There was a lot of white space in the notebook. Only sixty pages had writing on them, and some had precious little. The handwriting appeared to be Vail's, but occasionally the script turned larger and sloppier, as it did on the final page. When the journal was published—and Claire was sure it would be—it would make a very slim book. The size wouldn't matter to Vail scholars. To them the journal would be an electrical charge from a phantom limb, Jonathan Vail's message from another era.

Once the copies were made, Claire wanted to return to her office, lock the door, close the blinds, turn off the phone, shut down the computer and read, but she picked up the copies, the notebook, and the briefcase and carried them down the hall to the director's office. She was still wearing the white gloves, an obvious indication that she was holding an important docu-ment, even to an administrator as obtuse as Harrison Hough, who, at the moment, was talking to a colleague. Claire stood outside the doorway and waited until they finished their conversation. Harrison had the only office at the center with exterior windows. They were high up, near the ceiling, and while the sky could be seen through them, students walking by could not. When it turned dark, Claire had the impression a black cat rubbed its back against the glass. As soon as the colleague, Ralph Monroe, said good-bye to the director and headed for the door, Harrison glanced at his watch.

"That looks important," Ralph said, indicating the briefcase.

"It is," Claire replied.

She entered the office, closed the door behind her, and walked across the room, feeling as if she was about to hand Harrison a birthday cake made out of dust and paper and hide. He was given to subtle displays. His eyes widened slightly and he dropped the paper clip he'd been fiddling with, making Claire wish all over again that his predecessor was sitting in the director's chair.

"What's that?" he asked.

"I believe it's Jonathan Vail's missing journal."

"No!"

"Yes. A graduate student just brought it to me. He said he found it in a cave near Slickrock Canyon."

"Which graduate student?"

"Tim Sansevera."

"Never heard of him." Harrison's long, pale hands reached across his desk. "Let me see. I have some familiarity with Vail's handwriting."

"You should wear white gloves to look at the original, Harrison."

"I don't have a pair."

"Then let me show it to you. In addition to being one of *the* literary finds of this half of the century, the journal could be evidence in a criminal investigation."

Claire stood beside Harrison's desk and opened the notebook to the first page.

"What an incredible coup," Harrison said. "We'll be the envy of every center in the Southwest." He read the first entry. "The paper and ink appear old enough, and the writing could be Vail's. What do you think?" he asked, acknowledging rather tardily, Claire thought, that she was an expert.

She turned to the last page. "I think it's his, but the writing changes now and then. We will have to have it authenticated."

"The press will want to publish it, if it is Vail's."

"We'll need the family's permission."

"They've been generous and cooperative so far. Otto doesn't speak since he had his stroke. I know Ada well. She's a member of Friends of the Library. I'll talk to her. We should keep this discovery quiet until I do."

"We need to contact the rangers at Grand Gulch. Jonathan's disappearance is not an active investigation, but it's a case that was never solved."

"Would you take care of that?"

"All right."

"What do you think of this Tim . . . ?"

"Sansevera."

"Can we trust him? Could this be a theft or a hoax?"

"I've given Tim the Vail papers several times. He's doing his dissertation on Jonathan. I don't know him well, but I doubt he's a thief. What motive could he have for a hoax?"

Harrison's impatient shrug implied that that was all too obvious. "Career advancement," he said.

Claire hated to part with the original and the dusty briefcase, but Harrison insisted on locking them up in his office. She left one copy with him, took the others back to her office, and did what she had been wanting to do ever since Tim Sansevera showed up—hole up and read the journal. It resembled eating at a five-star restaurant for the first time or seeing a movie of a book she loved. Reality would have a hard time living up to anticipation.

Claire's inclination was to read for style first, then for content. The handwriting seemed to be Jonathan's under normal conditions, and occasionally Jonathan's under duress. It was his elliptical style with flashes of dazzling description. But there were fewer of these passages than she would have expected and more than she cared to know about the beans and rice he had eaten for dinner. Sometimes the writing seemed rushed, sometimes it seemed pedestrian, sometimes it seemed self-indulgent—but Jonathan had often seemed self-indulgent to Claire. There was nothing about Jennie Dell or about Jonathan's plans, although he did explain what he was doing in Slickrock Canyon. "Hiding out in the canyonlands. Trying to get my head together. Hoping they'll never find me."

"Who?" Claire wondered before moving on to the next entry.

"Haunted by what happened to Lou." Much as she knew about Jonathan, Claire did not know who Lou was.

There were numerous references to the fucking war, the bitch, and the fucking old lady. Claire feared that this was Jonathan's mother, Ada Vail, who was known to be imperious. Insulting her could make publication difficult. Claire wondered which would come first with Ada—the need to preserve her son's legend or the need to preserve her reputation. Publication didn't appear to have been on Jonathan's mind when he wrote the journal, but the pressure to publish now would be intense. Publication might do his legend a disservice, but even if it wasn't published, the journal was likely to be read and reread. Much would be seen in it that might not have been intended.

Claire felt that the first reading could be the purest reading. She tried to make her mind a blank slate before approaching the notebook. Once it had been read by others, her own reading might be influenced by their interpretations. When she finished, she put down the Xeroxed copy of the journal and considered what she had learned. There was little to advance Jonathan's reputation as a writer or a person, but much to harm it; possible clues to the riddle of his disappearance, but no solution; many questions, no answers. Jonathan's life and disappearance remained a puzzle.

Claire looked up the number for the Grand Gulch Ranger Station, called and asked to speak to Curt Devereux, the ranger who had investigated Jonathan's disappearance in 1966. She didn't expect Devereux to be at Grand Gulch after all this time, but his was the only name she had. When a woman answered the phone, Claire introduced herself and asked for Curt.

"I'm Ellen Frank," the woman said. "Curt is in the Gallup office now. I can give you his number there if you like."

"Please," said Claire.

Claire wrote the number down, then said, "I'm an archivist at the Center for Southwest Research at the University of New Mexico. Are you familiar with the legend of Jonathan Vail?"

"Somewhat," Ellen answered. "We sell his novel and his journal at the ranger station. They're popular with backpackers. Not as popular as Abbey, but people still like to read them."

"A student just brought me a notebook he found in Sin Nombre Canyon that appears to be Vail's missing journal."

"You're kidding. After all this time? Is it in good shape?"

"Excellent."

"The student should have brought it to us. It's not an active investigation, but Vail's disappearance is a case that has never been solved."

"I told the student that. He also found a duffel bag, which he left in the cave. I'm sure it will be of interest to whoever is conducting the investigation. Do you know who that would be?"

"I'm not sure, actually. That case has been inactive for so long. I know whoever it is will want to see the notebook. Can I get back to you?"

"Of course."

Claire hung up, then dialed the number she had been given for Curt Devereux. She had never met him but was curious about the man who'd been in the eye of the storm that swirled around Jonathan's disappearance. Claire explained who she was and why she was calling. There was a pause. Curt cleared his throat and said, "My God. After all this time. Do you believe the journal is authentic?"

"It appears to be, but we intend to have it authenticated by the family and a handwriting expert."

"I always wondered if Vail might have ended up in one of the side canyons. I've been all over Sin Nombre, but never found a trace."

"The student who brought it to me said he thought the cave had been covered by a rock slide and uncovered by another slide."

"That's possible. What's the student's name?"

"Tim Sansevera. He's a Ph.D. candidate writing his dissertation on Jonathan Vail."

"It used to be that students visited me, but I haven't spoken to one in years. Sansevera shouldn't have taken the journal out of the cave. It's not old enough to fall under the Antiquities Act, but it is evidence in an investigation that has never been closed."

"That's what Ellen Frank said. She told me she didn't know who would be in charge of the investigation at this point."

"I've got less than a year left here. I've been thinking about Jonathan Vail since the sixties. I sure would love to close my career out by finding out what happened to him. Thanks for calling. Someone from here will be in touch."

2

Chapter Two

Claire lived in the foothills in an area of high desert vegetation—cholla and prickly pear blending into piñon and juniper as the elevation increased. The only deciduous trees in her neighborhood had been planted by developers and residents. Her rear windows gave her a close-up of the Sandia mountains, which sparkled like an effervescent wine in the sunset's afterglow and turned cold and surreal beneath the light of the moon. The view from the front of her house, across the city and into the dusty vastness of the West Mesa, was almost too large to appreciate, although the sunsets were spectacular. There were times when Claire preferred the walls, the vegetation, and the seclusion of her courtyard to either view.

When she got home that night, she put her copy of Jonathan's journal on the bench by her front door, picked up her cat, Nemesis, and walked through the house. The cat was gray, the carpeting was gray, the walls were off-white with a minimum of artwork and decoration. Her house was subtle and subdued, and Claire liked it that way.

It was like October, and there was enough of a chill in the air to contemplate lighting the first fire of the season. Claire had two choices—the wood fireplace in her living room and the gas stove in her bedroom. She decided on the gas; it was easier and cleaner. She went into the bedroom, clicked the remote, and watched the gas flames lick the ceramic logs. Then she went to the kitchen, where she cooked herself some frozen pasta for dinner, her favorite meal since her divorce. One advantage to being single was that she didn't have to make her husband a salad every single night. By the time she had finished eating, the stove had warmed her bedroom and the cat had warmed her bed.

She took the copy of the journal to bed, thinking she would read it one more time, but it lay on the bedside table while she stared at the fire and thought about Jonathan Vail. She had seen him only once, at an antiwar demonstration she attended while visiting a friend at UNM. It was in the early summer of 1966, right after her freshman year at U of A. Jonathan had finally graduated from UNM by then and had already published two books. *The Journal of Jonathan Vail*, a record of time he'd spent wandering in the canyonlands, was published in 1965. It had some beautiful nature writing and was far more polished than the recent discovery, but he'd had a chance to work on that book with an editor. *A Blue-Eyed Boy* was published in the winter of 1966. It didn't find its audience until after Jonathan disappeared that summer, but Claire read it when it came out. Even then, before she knew she would be an archivist, she read everything she could get her hands on about the Southwest.

A local band called Las Margaritas had played at the demonstration. They had a few years of notoriety and popularity in the Southwest before breaking up. Claire remembered Jonathan and Jennie Dell sitting on the stage. Jennie got up and danced with the band, swinging her long blond hair and tapping a tambourine. Jonathan remained seated, looking withdrawn and sullen. When he finally spoke, he mumbled. Claire wasn't sure if the slurred speech was an affectation or if he was under the influence of drugs or alcohol. He had been known to show up at book signings inebriated. It was a time when being incoherent was considered appealing, and there was something rebellious and attractive about the slightly built, blue-eyed boy with the thick brown hair falling across his forehead. His manner was intense. He swayed as he gripped the mike. Claire wasn't sitting close enough to see the blue eyes Jonathan was famous for, but she saw the reaction of other women in the audience, the adulation that male writers can provoke in women.

Jonathan was twenty-three then, and in a few more years he would have become ineligible for the draft. Speaking out in public risked attracting the attention of the draft board, but that was how Jonathan Vail had lived, taking every risk, accepting every challenge. There were times when Claire envied his recklessness and his courage.

She kept her word to Harrison and didn't mention the journal to anyone when she got to work in the morning. The only way she could do that was to hide in her office and avoid her coworkers. Whenever Harrison entered her office, Claire felt a shadow glide across her desk, an amorphous kind of eastern shadow, not the sharp one cast by the New Mexico sun. She could always feel his presence, but sometimes she hesitated before acknowledging it. He cleared his throat, which was the signal it was past time for her to look away from her computer screen.

"Harrison," she said. "Hello."

He liked to give the impression that he was too busy for pleasantries, getting right to the point. "I dropped a copy of the notebook by Ada Vail's house on my way home last night. She was, as you can well imagine, overwhelmed by the discovery."

"Of course." Harrison usually maintained that he was too busy to sit down, so Claire had stopped offering him a chair. She could have stood up herself and been on his level, but she didn't do it. Respect was granted or denied by subtle gestures in academia.

Harrison picked up a paperweight from Claire's desk and cradled it in his long white fingers. He had the fingers of a pianist, but Claire, who had been a musician herself, was convinced he had never played. Harrison didn't have a musical soul.

"Ada is an elderly woman," he said. "Still very active, but in her eighties. I feared the shock might be too much for her. After all, this was a message from the grave, from a son who has been gone and presumed dead for more than thirty years. She recovered well, however, thanked me profusely and said she would read the journal overnight." Harrison put the paper-weight down two inches from where he had picked it up. "She called me this morning. There were things she found disturbing in the journal. She wants to talk to you. I made an appointment for you to meet at her house at eleven-thirty."

Claire glanced at the time on her computer screen. "That's an hour from now, Harrison."

He placed his fingertips together, forming a tent, and pointed the tip of it at Claire. "Ada has been most generous to the center."

"I'm aware of that."

"We need the notebook to complete the Vail collection. I'm counting on you to keep Ada Vail happy."

"I'll do my best," Claire said, but she felt she would have been able to do a better job if she'd had time to prepare herself. Harrison had barely given her time to comb her hair before driving across town to the Vails'. Claire hated to be late, so she tended to arrive early. If it was her first visit, she might be as much as half an hour early, which often left her with time to kill driving around unfamiliar neighborhoods.

Today, she ended up ringing Ada Vail's doorbell at eleven-twenty. The Vails lived in a large house near the country club. The lawn, an intense, clipped green, was surrounded by pyracantha that had been trimmed to form a hedge. At this time of year, it was embellished with orange berries. Claire thought pyracantha was a nasty plant, full of thorns, but planting one beneath the window did keep intruders away. The Vails' street was lined with cottonwood trees that cast deep pools of shadow. It was quiet and verdant, a long way from the dust of Sin Nombre Canyon.

The doorbell was answered by a Mexican maid with features that Claire identified as Mayan.

"*Hola*," she said.

"*Buenas días*," the maid replied.

"Is Mrs. Vail home?"

"You are Señora Reynier?"

"Yes."

"Come inside," the maid replied. "She is expecting you."

Claire followed the maid into the living room, which had hardwood floors stained so dark they appeared burnt. It was a large room running the depth of the house, from the windows that faced the street to glass doors that opened onto the rear patio. The windows had pale blue velvet drapes that puddled where they landed on the floor. The room was large enough to have several groupings of furniture, each including a white sofa, a pair of matching armchairs, and a polished coffee table. The fireplace had ceramic logs and a glass door. While the maid went to get Ada Vail, Claire examined the painting centered over the fireplace, a moody brown landscape by Russell Chatham, a Montana artist she admired. The beauty of the painting and the money it took to buy it prompted the thought that an artist—like an archivist—has to please a few people who have a lot of money, and a writer has to please a lot of people who have a little money. Her job was to please Ada Vail so that the center could keep the journal in its collection and UNM Press could publish it. Although she admired the painting, Claire thought the rest of the room had the effect of new money trying to look like old money. There was too much crystal dangling from the chandelier, too much pale blue carpet with the matching drapes, too many ceramic figurines. It was the House That Felt Had Built.

Claire couldn't decide which cluster of furniture to sit on, so she walked to the rear of the room and stared out the window at the sprinklers watering the smooth-as-carpet lawn. The cushions had been removed from the wrought-iron patio furniture, making it look skeletal and forbidding.

She heard the sound of a wheelchair in the hallway and turned around to see a nurse in a uniform that stretched tight across her hips wheeling an elderly gentleman, presumably Otto Vail, into the room. "Mrs. Vail will be here shortly," the nurse said.

She wheeled Otto to the one group of furniture that lacked an armchair and left him there to complete the arrangement. Her rubber-soled shoes squeaked as she exited the room, leaving Claire in silence with Otto. Except for blue veins tunneling across the back of his hand, the stroke seemed to have drained the color from him. His thin hair was silvery, his skin the pallid white of flesh that has been wrapped in a Band-Aid or submerged underwater. He had a long, thin face, and his cavernous cheeks made Claire wonder if the nurse had neglected to insert his dentures. He brought silence into the room with him, yet his eyes blazed with an angry blue light. To get closer to his level, Claire sat down on the sofa.

She knew she was talking to fill the void and that even if Otto could hear, he couldn't respond, but the silence was so uncomfortable that she spoke anyway, trying to keep her voice to its normal cadence and pitch. "Hello, Mr. Vail," she said. "My name is Claire Reynier. I work at the Center for Southwest Research at UNM, and I'm the archivist for your son's collection. A grad student named Tim Sansevera brought me the journal that has been missing all these years. He found it in Sin Nombre Canyon a few days ago. It's a remarkable find."

Otto Vail looked exactly the same when she finished this introduction as he had when she started. Not a muscle had moved. His eyes continued to blaze. Claire understood there was no way of knowing what a stroke victim heard, yet she felt that Otto had listened to her. Was that her own ego talking or had he made some sign too subtle to be registered consciously? "The center is very happy to have Jonathan's papers. We deeply appreciate the family's generosity."

She heard the staccato beat of high heels in the hallway and stood up, mindful of her role as a representative of the center and the importance of pleasing Ada Vail. The object was to show intelligence and respect, but, she hoped, not to grovel. Ada Vail entered the room. Even in stiletto heels, she was a tiny woman, so tiny that she made Claire feel large and awkward.

There were many ways for a woman to age, and Claire knew that longevity didn't necessarily reward kindness and gentility. Often the women who remained fierce did best. Claire put Ada Vail in that category. Her hair was dyed black, parted in the middle and pulled back into a bun. It was an unforgiving style that accented her sharp brown eyes and prominent nose, and a high-maintenance color that would require frequent visits to the hairdresser. Ada wore bright-red lipstick and a red dress. The vivid colors and dyed hair made a statement. Not that she was young, but that she was vital.

"I am Ada Vail." She extended a bony hand that sparkled with diamonds.

"It's a pleasure to meet you," Claire said.

"Please, be seated. You have met Otto?"

"Yes."

She sat in the armchair facing her husband. "He doesn't hear a thing, but I try to include him." She turned toward her husband, raised her voice, and began to speak slowly and distinctly, as if she were talking to an infant—everything Claire had tried not to do. "Ms. Reynier came here to talk to us about Jonathan's journal. It has been found after all this time. Extraordinary, isn't it?" She turned back to Claire and resumed speaking in her normal voice. "Would you like anything? Coffee? Tea? Mineral water?"

"No, thank you," Claire said. "I've been admiring the painting." As her eyes turned toward the fireplace, she had the distinct impression that Otto's eyes followed hers. "I'm fond of Russell Chatham."

"He's a favorite of Otto's and mine." Ada turned toward her husband. "Isn't that right, Otto?" Otto gave no response. Now it appeared to Claire that his eyes were focused on the fireplace, burning as if they reflected a fire there. Ada turned back to

Claire. "It was so kind of Harrison to bring me Jonathan's journal last night. We have been dealing with the center for close to thirty years. Many people have come and gone in that time. I knew your predecessor, Irina, and I am very glad to finally meet you."

Was that an emphasis on the "finally"? Claire wondered. She had been wanting to meet Ada Vail since she took the job, but interacting with benefactors was an area that Harrison appropriated for himself.

"Personally I always found Harrison's predecessor . . . What was his name? Brett?"

"Burke. Burke Lovell."

"A brilliant man, I'm sure, but rather restless and unpredictable. Harrison strikes me as a courteous and steady person."

Harrison was steady as a stone, but courtesy was a side of him Claire had yet to see. Someone at the center had to coax generosity from the rich and the powerful. If Harrison was good at it, more power to him. Still, he had sent *her* on this mission.

"Harrison tells me that UNM is interested in publication, and that, as the archivist, you would be the liaison with them."

"I would love to see the journal published," Claire admitted.

"You must know a great deal about Jonathan by now."

"Only what has been written by him and about him. I certainly don't know him as you do." It was as close as Claire could bring herself to flattering Ada Vail.

"He was our son." Ada glanced at Otto. "But Jonathan had some strange companions after he got involved in the antiwar movement." Her eyes took on an intensity that equaled her husband's. Claire had an image of them in a dark room, two pairs of eyes glaring, like those of predatory animals. "The drugs, the hippie friends. There were sides to Jonathan that I never understood. I come from a military family. We sold our products to the government, and we always supported the war effort. In my family the men went to war. They didn't dodge the draft."

Claire had nothing to say. She thought the unjustness of the Vietnam War was an issue that had been settled long ago. It hadn't occurred to her that for some people it never would be settled.

"You are quite sure this journal was written by my son and is not a forgery?" Ada asked.

"If it's a forgery, it's a very skillful one."

"I'm not convinced that all the ideas expressed are my son's."

"We'll have it authenticated by an expert," Claire reassured her.

"Make that your first step, then we will decide what to do about publication. If this is Jonathan's work, there are passages I intend to excise before it can be published."

That was what Claire had feared she would say. It would take a very understanding mother to allow publication of a book that referred to her as a fucking old lady. Claire didn't see a lot of understanding in Ada's straight back and severe expression. She attempted to keep her voice sympathetic without being craven. "I understand how you feel, but scholars will view this as a historical document and will want it published exactly as it is."

Ada looked Claire right in the eye and said, "I won't allow that."

Claire moved on to the next sensitive issue. "We would like to keep the original at the center, if that suits you. We can preserve it there, under optimum conditions."

"That would be acceptable," Ada said.

"How do you feel about access?" When Ada and Otto had

donated Jonathan's other papers to the center, they limited access to scholars, which was a donor's right.

"At the moment I'd like to limit access to the handwriting expert and to people who actually work at the center. No students. No press."

"Would you have any objection to my showing a copy to the grad student who found the journal? He was very careful not to damage the original by reading it. He is doing his dissertation on Jonathan. It would be one way of thanking him for bringing the journal to us."

Ada twisted a diamond ring on her finger. She deliberated for a minute, then said, "That would be all right."

"There is also the issue of the government investigation," Claire said.

"What investigation? They did precious little, if you ask me," replied Ada, looking out the window at a gardener as he snipped off a couple of wandering pyracantha branches. "I had to hire my own private investigator, Nick Lorenz."

"Even so, the case was never solved, and the center was legally obligated to report the find to the ranger station in Grand Gulch as evidence."

"Did you see anything in that journal that would explain the disappearance of my son?"

"No. Did you?"

"No. After years of having Nick track down leads that went nowhere, I finally concluded that my son was murdered. In my mind, the prime suspect has always been Jennie Dell. The federal government bungled the investigation the first time. Why give them the chance to do it again?"

"If we refuse to show it to them, they could get a subpoena. It's possible they'll see some clue in the journal that you and I missed. The reference to Lou, for example. Do you know who that is?"

"No. Show it to them if you must, but no one else, certainly not the press."

"All right," Claire agreed.

"Is there anything else? Otto appears to be getting tired."

Otto looked exactly the same to Claire as he had when he entered the room. "Would you like to come to the center to see the original document?" she asked.

"Let me think about it." Ada stood up and extended her hand. "Thank you for your time."

"Thank you," Claire replied.

3

Chapter Three

Claire stopped at Duran's Pharmacy on Central for lunch. She sat at the counter and ate tamales, enjoying their texture and heat. When she got back to the center she noticed a man standing beside the reception desk. He didn't have a hat, but she had the fleeting impression that he held one in front of him. It seemed like the kind of gesture this man would make. He wore a short-sleeved shirt, a bolo tie, and khaki pants that were belted above his stomach. He was at least six feet tall and over two hundred pounds, but his posture was deferential. He gave the impression he was waiting for someone, and Claire suspected she was the someone. She had heard a lot about the kind of person Curt Devereux was, but little about his appearance. Yet her instinct told her this was what he looked like.

Claire walked up to him, introduced herself, and asked if he was Curt Devereux.

"How did you know?" he asked.

"I made an educated guess," Claire replied. "I've read a lot about you." Even after she introduced herself, Curt continued to give the impression he was waiting for something. Retirement? Claire wondered. Waiting for retirement went with the territory when a person worked for the federal government. It could be dangerous, Claire thought, to wait until middle age to start living your life. She had recently been through the death of a parent, the death of a mentor, and a divorce. She had come out of that turbulent period with the conviction that life had to be lived every moment, as it happened. She looked into Curt Devereux's unblinking eyes and placid face. If he felt anger or regret about his career or about anything else, he concealed it well.

"Let's go to my office," Claire said.

"This is a wonderful building," Curt told her. "It's everything a library should be."

Claire agreed with him. Zimmerman Library had been designed by the architect John Gaw Meem and was beautifully proportioned, with high ceilings supported by rows of vigas and corbels. "Have you been here before?" she asked as she opened the wrought-iron door that led to the center's offices.

"I worked in the Park Service office in Albuquerque in the seventies. I used to come in and study the Vail papers to see if I could find any clues to Jonathan's disappearance in his writing. I know the journal and *A Blue-Eyed Boy* are available in print, but those versions had been edited and they weren't in Vail's handwriting. I thought I might find something in the originals. Maybe I just liked coming here. I always felt I'd like to get a Ph.D."

"In what?"

"History."

They had reached Claire's office. "You have time," she said as she opened the door, but she knew well enough that some men retired and died before they ever had a chance to fulfill their dreams.

"As I told you, I have less than a year left with the federal government," Curt replied. "Lately I've been pushing papers around and serving out my term, but I pulled some strings and managed to get myself reassigned to the Vail case. It will be getting attention again now that the journal has been found. The federal government doesn't like to concede that a person can vanish without a trace on public lands. They'd still like to know what happened to Jonathan Vail, and nothing would give me greater satisfaction than to end my career by finding out. May I?" He gestured toward the visitor's chair in front of Claire's desk.

"Please."

As he bent forward to ease himself into the chair Claire noticed that the hair on top of his head was thin and his scalp was freckled and pink. She sat down herself.

"I assume you've read the journal?" Curt asked.

"I have," Claire replied.

"Will I find anything there that will solve the mystery?" He smiled.

"I'd rather you read it before we talk about it. I think it's best to read it with as blank a slate as possible."

"All right," Curt agreed. "Well, let's get on with it. Is the document in the Anderson Reading Room?"

"I'll bring it to you there."

Claire went down the hall to Harrison's office. His interest in the journal had already turned proprietary. Suspicion came easily to him. "Who wants to see it?" he demanded.

"Curt Devereux, the ranger who conducted the initial investigation. He's been put back on the case."

Harrison reluctantly handed over the briefcase, and Claire took it to the reading room. Curt knew the drill and had already surrendered his ID to Gail Benton, the librarian who manned the reference desk. He had put on his white gloves and was sitting rather demurely, Claire thought, at a table.

"Ah," he said when she handed it to him, "canyon dust."

"Ada Vail wants to restrict access to law enforcement and staff. She feels that the notebook should not leave the center."

"I don't have any problem with that. I would like a copy to take with me, however."

"I'll make one for you," Claire said.

Curt fingered the thick hide. "What kind of leather is this? Do you know?"

"No," Claire replied.

She made another Xerox copy for Devereux, then went back to her office to wait for his reaction. By now she had read the journal several times, but her first impression hadn't changed. Ruth O'Connor, a coworker who had noticed Curt in her office, stopped by to ask who he was. Claire had kept *her* word to Harrison not to talk about the journal, but *his* resolve appeared to have lasted about five minutes. It was the day after the discovery, and word was all over the center. Anyone seen visiting Claire now was presumed to be connected to the journal.

Ruth reminded Claire of an alert little bird. She was the oldest member of the department, but retirement was not in her vocabulary. She enjoyed what she was doing far too much. Her eyes were sharp behind her trifocal lenses. She had a way of tipping her head when she talked, as if she were trying to find the right viewpoint in the glasses. "Who was that guy?" she asked Claire, poking her head through the door.

"What guy?" Claire responded, even though she knew full well who Ruth was talking about.

"The big one—Smokey the Bear."

"Curt Devereux, the ranger who investigated the disappearance of Jonathan Vail way back when. He's still with the Park Service and is reopening the case. He's in the Anderson Reading Room examining the notebook."

"Isn't that just like the federal government?" asked Ruth. "A man messes up an investigation once, and thirty years later they give him the opportunity to mess it up all over again."

"How do you know that Curt messed up the first time?"

"He didn't find Jonathan Vail, did he?"

"No." Claire resisted the assumption, common around universities, that academics were smarter than everyone else. But Ruth believed she'd proven her point and went back to her office.

Curt Devereux returned sooner than Claire expected, sat down, and made himself comfortable.

"What do you think?" she asked him.

"It looks like Vail's writing, except for the places where it gets large and sloppy."

"He might have been under stress."

"He could also have been on drugs. He was a known user."

"It could explain the reference to La Sagrada Familia."

"The sacred family. I thought that was an ironic reference to his own family."

"Possibly. It's also an unfinished church in Barcelona. The masonry walls seem to be sliding off the frame, which is the way some people perceive things when they're on LSD." Claire had taken LSD while traveling through Europe with her lover, Pietro, in 1967 and 1968. At the time she thought it explained the artistic vision of some artists, including Vincent van Gogh and Antonio Gaudí.

Curt didn't question her about LSD, which was all right with Claire. She had no desire to be discussing thirty-year-old acid trips in her office. On the other hand, Curt showed a remarkable lack of curiosity for an investigator.

"The style of the journal also seems to be Vail's," he said.

"I'd say so, but it's not up to the standard set by *A Blue-Eyed Boy*," Claire replied.

"I'll let you be the judge of that. I was reading more for content myself. This is the first I've heard of Lou. Do you know who he is?"

"No," Claire admitted. "I was rather surprised that Jennie Dell was never mentioned, since she was with Jonathan in the canyon."

"She claims she got there on the tenth. She signed in at the ranger station that day. I never found anything to contradict her story. There were only a few entries after she got to Slickrock."

"She *was* his girlfriend. You'd think he'd have had some thoughts about her."

"Vail was a self-centered individual. He was concerned about getting his draft notice and angry at his folks for not getting him a deferment."

"Would they really have been able to?"

"It wasn't unheard of for prominent businessmen to get deferments for their employees. The Vails sold their products to the army. They were major contributors to the Republican Party. They had influence." Curt leaned forward in his chair, resting his bear-paw hands on his knees. "I never thought the family gave Jennie her due. She was always very cooperative with the investigation."

The light in Curt's eyes when he talked about Jennie set off an alarm in Claire. A middle-aged man investing power in a younger woman, she thought. Of course, Curt hadn't been middle-aged when he'd known Jennie Dell. He had probably been the same age as she, but he was a ranger and Jennie was a footloose hippie.

"She was a good-looking woman," Curt said, "with long blond hair down to her waist. Jonathan Vail didn't appreciate what he had. Did you make me a copy of the journal?"

"Yes." Claire handed it over.

"I'll reread it, but I hope I'll find more in the cave than I did in the journal. I'll need to contact Tim Sansevera."

Claire supplied his address and phone number.

"I want to see exactly where he found the briefcase, and I'll need to examine the duffel bag and to see if there is any other evidence in the cave. You know as much about Vail as anyone. Would you be interested in going to Sin Nombre with Sansevera and me?"

Claire wondered whether this was proper procedure, but she was delighted to be asked. "I'd love to," she said.

"How is your schedule?"

"No problem. I could go anytime this week or over the weekend."

"I'll set it up for Saturday." Curt stood up and gave Claire's hand a firm shake. "It will be a pleasure to work with you."

"I'm looking forward to it," said Claire.

When Tim came by the next morning to pick up his photocopy, he was wearing jeans and a T-shirt, possibly even the same jeans and T-shirt he'd had on when Claire had seen him a few days ago. But today his clothes were clean, and he wasn't covered with a layer of dust, although his running shoes seemed to be tinted permanently pink.

"Did Curt Devereux get in touch with you?" Claire asked him.

"He came to my place." Claire had deduced from Tim's address that he lived in the student ghetto. "We're meeting at the trailhead to Slickrock Canyon."

"I'm going, too," Claire said.

"Are you?" Tim replied, with an expression in his green eyes that Claire couldn't read. "What did you think of the guy?"

Claire, who hadn't made up her mind yet, chose her words carefully. "He seemed agreeable."

"Agreeable!" Tim's lips started to form an expletive, but then he remembered that he was a graduate student and Claire was an assistant professor. "He's a potato head."

"Excuse me?"

"You know the kid's toy where you stick plastic face parts onto a real potato? Devereux puts on the right expression for every occasion, but basically the guy's a blank."

"He's preparing to retire from the federal government. Most likely he's spent most of his working life concealing his thoughts."

"If he ever had any to conceal. I don't have a lot of confidence in him. I'd never trust a man who wears his pants around his armpits."

When a man has a stomach, his pants have to go somewhere, Claire thought.

"If someone discovers what happened to Jonathan Vail, it won't be Curt Devereux. Did you find any clues in the journal?"

"Let's talk about that after you read it," Claire said. "I think it's better to approach the journal without preconceptions." She suspected, however, that Tim's interest was too proprietary to allow him to approach anything related to Jonathan Vail without preconceptions. "Ada Vail gave me permission to give you a photocopy, but she is restricting access to people who work at the center. Please don't show this to anyone." She gave the photocopy to Tim and watched while he put it into his backpack.

"I won't," he said. "Did you mention publication to Ada Vail?"

"Yes. There are things in the journal she wants to suppress."

"She can't suppress a word," Tim cried. Once again Claire had the sensation that he was radiating canyon heat. "The journal has to be published exactly as it is."

Claire wondered if this was the moment to tell him that it wasn't his decision to make—but she decided against it. She was meeting with an editor at UNM Press that afternoon, but there were many issues to be resolved before publication could even be considered.

"I'll see you in Slickrock Canyon," she said. "I'm looking forward to it."

"Me, too," Tim said, hoisting his backpack.

Other than getting around the UNM campus, people seldom walked in Albuquerque, or in Tucson either, where Claire had lived and worked before coming to the center. By the time the sun rose, it was too hot to walk in Tucson, but people didn't have that excuse in Albuquerque, where the nights and mornings were always cool. Claire had been too rushed to do her tai chi this morning and needed some exercise, so she walked to the UNM Press office, where she had an appointment with an editor named Avery Dunstan. She passed through the exhibition room and went out the front door of the center. The bicycle rack had a sign that had once read, LEAVE YOUR BICYCLES AND E-Z GO CARTS OUTSIDE but had been vandalized to read, LEAVE YOUR TESTICLES AND EGOS OUTSIDE. Advice that was seldom followed in a university.

She walked around the west side of the building, stopping for a minute beside the duck pond and noticing the way the tower reflected across the surface. The center's massive walls made it seem solid and grounded, but its tower reached for the sky. It was the university's signature building—a good place to store rare manuscripts.

Claire walked west to University and north to Lomas, where UNM Press was located in an undistinguished strip-mall building. Whenever she came to this office, she was glad she worked at the beautiful center, although she suspected there might be more camaraderie among the editors at the press than there was among the librarians. She gave her name to the receptionist and waited for Avery.

"Claire," he called as he came rushing down the hall, reminding her of a long-legged bird that, no matter how much it flapped its wings, never got off the ground. Avery was in his mid-thirties, Claire guessed, six feet tall and thin as a reed. His brown hair was tousled, and he wore khaki pants and a white shirt. One eye was slightly crossed, which gave him a permanently puzzled expression.

"Excellent to see you," he said, giving Claire a hug.

"Good to see you, Avery," she replied.

"I am so incredibly excited about Jonathan Vail's journal! Let's go back to my office where we can discuss it."

Claire felt there was no privacy to be had in the press's office cubicles, so you might as well talk in the hallway as anywhere else, but she followed Avery to his office, passing a cubicle that appeared to be a graveyard for dead computers. A screen saver was doing loops on Avery's computer monitor, and pictures of a solemn-faced woman were taped to his walls. The woman was Avery's wife, Heather, whom Claire had met at the press's annual Christmas party. Avery's flamboyant manner contrasted with Heather's steady, quiet presence.

Avery picked up his copy of Jonathan's journal and hugged it to his chest before putting it back on his desk. "This is the find of a lifetime. A lifetime! We will be ever so lucky if it doesn't go to a New York publisher."

"What do you think of the writing?" Claire asked him.

"Honestly? Between you and me?" he said in a stage whisper, glancing surreptitiously around his cubicle.

And anyone else who happens to be listening, Claire thought. "Honestly," she replied.

"Leaden. Flat. But he was out there in the wilderness scribbling by a campfire, right? It's not great literature, but it is Jonathan Vail, so who cares?"

"Now *you* sound like a New York publisher."

"We consider this to be a book with historical significance that we definitely want to publish, but first we will have to get permission from whoever holds the rights."

"Presumably that's the parents, and they could be difficult. The father has been incapacitated by a stroke, and there's no telling what he thinks. The mother is already talking about cutting out passages she doesn't like."

"She can't!" Avery cried, throwing up his hands in exasperation. "The journal is a historical document that needs to be published exactly as it is. Personally I would not change one single word. Can you talk to her?"

"I tried. I didn't get very far."

"I'll talk to her, then," said Avery.

Claire didn't think that Ada would be receptive to the flamboyant Avery. "She is very conservative," Claire replied.

"There's always the rumor that Jonathan left behind a child. If there is such a child and anyone can find him or her, there's an heir. I know for a fact that royalties for *A Blue-Eyed Boy* are paid to Jennie Dell."

"How do you know that?"

"I talked to the editor in New York once about doing a limited edition of that book, and she told me. Jonathan had some arrangement with Jennie. Maybe he left her the rights to the journal, too. I'm counting on you, Claire, to get the matter settled. If we publish, we want you to write the foreword and to annotate our edition."

It was a considerable honor. "I'd love to," Claire said.

"You deserve to," Avery replied. "You're his archivist. Having your name on Jonathan Vail's journal will add enormous prestige to your career. It will be a ten without a doubt." Archivists and librarians were graded each year for librarianship, research and publication, and university community service, ten points in each category. Claire needed some publication points this year. "And I know that with your name on it you'll want to get permission to publish the manuscript intact."

"Tim Sansevera, the grad student who found the manuscript, wants to see his name on it."

"A grad student?" Avery's errant eye did a loop around the ceiling and settled on his nose. Grad students didn't get their name on a book if a professor was involved, no matter how much they contributed—which had more to do with ego than merit or effort. Claire didn't actually teach, but she was still considered a member of the faculty and held the title of assistant professor. "Mention him in the acknowledgments," Avery said. It was the standard method of dealing with grad students.

"He won't be content with that."

"Does he have a choice? Finding a manuscript in a cave doesn't constitute ownership. Talk to him. Work it out. You can do it."

Claire wasn't so sure. Her mood was reflected in her posture as she left Avery's office and walked across the campus. Hunched over like Kokopelli, the Anasazi flute player, she felt as though she was toting a backpack that was filled with stones.

4

Chapter Four

When Claire answered her phone later that afternoon the voice on the line sounded hesitant and husky. "I'd like to speak to Claire Reynier?" the caller whispered, putting a question mark where there should have been a period.

"I'm Claire Reynier."

"This is Jennie Dell." The image that came to Claire's mind was of the hippie with long blond hair beating a tambourine on a stage. She was too startled to respond immediately. Jennie hesitated, too, then said, "Curt Devereux gave me a copy of Jonathan's journal."

"He did?" Claire asked, adding a question mark of her own. It was a lame response, but she needed time to think. She didn't believe Curt should be showing the journal to a woman who had once been a suspect.

"It was a shock to see it after all this time."

"I'm sure it was."

"Curt said that UNM is considering publication?"

"It's under consideration, but there are a lot of issues that need to be resolved—rights, for one thing."

"Ada Vail can be difficult."

Claire had nothing to add to that. There was another lengthy pause in the conversation. "Where are you calling from?" she finally asked, to fill the vacuum.

"Madrid. I live here now."

Claire knew by the emphasis on the first syllable that Jennie was talking about the former mining town southwest of Santa Fe, not the city in Spain.

"Curt told me you're meeting him in Slickrock Canyon on Saturday?"

Claire resisted the impulse to say, "He did?" again. She was bothered by Curt's lack of discretion and confidentiality. The fact that this was an old investigation didn't make it insignificant in her mind. To her what happened to Jonathan Vail was very significant. As an archivist, she knew that a rumor that gets repeated often enough becomes accepted as fact. She had heard all the rumors about Curt's incompetence, but she needed facts to believe them. So far he seemed to be doing his best to live up to his reputation. "Did he invite you to come along, too?" she asked, hoping that he hadn't.

"No, he didn't, but I wouldn't have gone even if he had. I have no desire to return to that place ever again. Besides . . . " She laughed. "I've become a house cat. I was wondering if you could stop by here on your way? I'd like to talk to you about the notebook and what would be in Jonathan's best interests. I'm not hard to find—it's the yellow house with turquoise trim on the west side of town. Follow the dirt road next to the glassblowers."

Claire agreed. She was intrigued by the thought of meeting the woman who had existed for so long as a character on a page, a character considered duplicitous by some, honorable by others. Curt Devereux had come out of the Vail investigation with a tarnished reputation, but Jennie's remained ambiguous.

Claire left the center Friday afternoon prepared for hiking in Grand Gulch. She had good boots. She brought along a hat, sunscreen, a day pack, lots of water, and trail mix. She worried about keeping up with Curt and Tim, who spent a lot more time in the wilderness than she did. Tai chi, which had taught her how to keep an opponent off balance by embracing the opposite, was good preparation for her job at the center, but she didn't know if it could prepare her for the wilderness, or for Jennie Dell either.

She took the back road to Madrid, passing through Tijeras Canyon on the section of I-40 where trucks picked up speed for the long haul to Amarillo. She got off at Cedar Crest and turned north onto Highway 14, the old Turquoise Trail. From an Albuquerque resident's point of view this was the back side of the Sandia Mountains. The west side was high desert. The east side was green with piñon, juniper, and cedar. It had rained recently. The sky was heavy with clouds, and there were places where gravel had washed across the highway.

Development moved relentlessly north on Route 14. The farther north Claire drove, the larger the houses and building lots became. She took a deep breath and exhaled when she passed San Pedro Creek, the last development, and entered the place that was described in a Spanglish road sign as El Corazón del Ortiz Ranch. KEEP OUT was painted on tires attached periodically to a fence. It was a beautiful and valuable property located midway between Albuquerque and Santa Fe. From here on, the road passed through ranch country and ghost towns.

Claire drove through Golden admiring the rounded lines of the whitewashed adobe church. Adobe always gave her the impression that it was rising out of the earth at the same time that it was sinking back in. Ten miles later she rounded a curve and came upon the slag heap that marked the entrance to the former mining town of Madrid. It was one of the rare towns in New Mexico that had little natural beauty. Claire couldn't remember when Madrid was an active mining town, but she remembered when in the seventies, artists and craftspeople who could no longer afford to live in Santa Fe began fixing up the abandoned board-and-batten miners' shacks and moving in. Some had been painted, some were weathered stony gray, some were too far gone to ever be restored, reduced to skeletons. Madrid had once been a very lonely place, but now the mainstreet bustled with restaurants and shops, and finding a parking space could be a challenge. Claire followed Jennie's directions and turned onto a dirt road that was pockmarked with potholes and ruts. The recent rain had left puddles in the holes. Going five miles an hour and dodging the puddles, Claire came to the yellow house with turquoise trim that belonged to Jennie. Next to it a weathered shed functioned as a garage. The door was open, and Claire could see a compact car inside that matched the turquoise trim. She parked in the driveway and walked to the front door. The doorbell was a wind chime, a series of graduated metal pipes. Claire struck it, and the sound reverberated along the pipes.

When the door opened and she faced Jennie Dell, the woman who was nearly as legendary as Jonathan Vail, Claire had the sensation that the front door was the cover of a pop-up book and that Jennie was popping out of the pages. She had put on about twenty pounds but was still an attractive woman, an earth mother now instead of a sprite. Her abundant blond hair rippled down her back, but silver framed her face. She wore an ankle-length denim dress with a scoop neck that showed ample cleavage. The dress had long sleeves that were narrow at the shoulder but full at the wrist. When Jennie raised her arms Claire could see that the sleeves had a yellow lining. Jennie reminded her of Stevie Nicks in her latest, full-figure incarnation.

"I'm Jennie," she said in her husky voice.

"Claire Reynier."

"You found the house all right?"

"The turquoise trim helped."

Jennie laughed. "Come on in." She picked up a butterscotch-colored cat with white paws that had leapt onto the doorstep the minute Claire struck the chime. "This is Butterscotch. You're not allergic to cats, are you?"

"No. I have one myself."

"You look like a cat person."

Jennie put the cat down on the wood floor, and Claire followed her into the house, which had a fragrant, smoky smell as if someone had walked through it waving a smudge stick. Burning sage was a ritual practiced in New Mexico to cleanse a house of bad thoughts or to conceal offensive odors.

"My son says that if there is reincarnation he wants to come back as a single woman's cat. No other being in the universe gets as much attention," Claire said.

"Smart man," Jennie replied.

Claire realized she didn't know whether Jennie was single or not. "Are you single?" she asked.

"Yes," said Jennie. "And you?"

"Recently divorced."

"Ah," said Jennie. "Can I get you something? An herb tea?"

"That would be fine," Claire said.

Jennie went into the kitchen, and Claire sat down in the living room, which relied heavily on Guatemalan fabric for decoration. Or was that overdecoration? Huipils were thumbtacked to the walls. The cushions on the sofa and chairs were a red-striped fabric. There were numerous embroidered pillows, and a wicker basket full of cloth dolls in native dress. The room was small and busy. The dominant color was red. It was a contrast to Claire's spare, subdued house, but once she got used to it, she rather liked it. Long enough for a visit, anyway.

Jennie came back with a tray holding an earthenware tea pot and two cups. She put the tray down on the wicker basket she used as a coffee table and sat down on the red sofa, arranging her dress so that the skirt spread across the cushions. It occurred to Claire that she had dressed to complement the room. Denim blue was about the only color one could get away with in here.

"Do you work for Maya Jones?" she asked. It was a store in Madrid that sold Guatemalan imports.

Jennie leaned back against the cushions. "No, but I buy a lot of stuff there. I'm a writer."

"What do you write?"

"Mini books. Those little books you see beside the checkout counter in the bookstores? I do different subjects. Dogs, astrology, food. It's a living." She laughed. "I guess. I published a novel once, but it didn't do well."

It was an entrée to a subject Claire wanted to discuss. "I've been talking to UNM Press about publishing Jonathan's journal. Avery Dunstan, the editor I work with there, heard from Jonathan's editor in New York that the royalties for *A Blue-Eyed Boy* go to you."

"They do," Jennie said. "After he received his draft notice, Jonathan made a written request so that if anything happened to him, I would get the royalties. His parents didn't object, and the publisher honored the request. Jonathan never had a formal will. All he had to leave were his royalties and his truck. The royalties supported me for a while, but eventually sales fell off. I couldn't afford to live in Santa Fe anymore, so I moved out here."

"But you and Jonathan never married?"

"Never," Jennie said, pouring the tea. "Why do you ask?"

"The rumor persists that he left an heir."

"A lot of rumors persist about Jonathan. I wish *that* one were true—or at least that he'd left an heir by me, but he didn't. And if he'd had a child by someone else I believe I would have known."

"Another persistent rumor is that he didn't die in the canyonlands. That somewhere in the world Jonathan Vail is alive and well."

Jennie handed Claire her cup of tea. "Ada would have found him if that were true. She paid her private investigator, Nick Lorenz, a fortune, and he made finding Jonathan his life's work. That man hounded Jonathan and me."

Claire took a sip of her tea, which had the dark, spicy flavor of Emperor's Choice. "Jonathan's parents have the rights to the journal unless there's a document or a child out there to prove otherwise."

"As far as I know, there isn't. What has Ada decided to do with it?"

"She is leaving the original at the center for the time being, accessible only to staff and law enforcement."

"She's not going to like being called the fucking old lady," Jennie said with a laugh.

The only experience Claire had had with law enforcement had to do with library thefts, but it seemed to her that Curt had gone beyond the scope of his investigation by giving Jennie a copy of the journal, particularly since he knew Ada Vail had restricted access. "Why did Curt give you a copy of the journal?" she asked.

"He wanted me to take some time to study it and see if I found anything that could help the investigation. He always believed that what I heard and saw in Slickrock Canyon was the truth. Unlike some people, he didn't doubt me."

Jennie raised an arm to brush her hair out of her face, and her sleeve fell open, revealing the yellow lining of her dress. She looked like a sorceress, and Claire was reminded of the fascination some women in the sixties had with the occult. She could understand how the vivid Jennie could cast a spell over the plain Curt. She lived in Technicolor. He lived in khaki.

"Have you and Curt kept in touch?" she asked.

"We did at first, but it has been years since I saw him. He was curious about some things in the journal. He had never heard of Lou and wondered who he was."

"I wondered that myself."

"His full name is Lou Bastiann. He was a fan of Jonathan's. You've read *A Blue-Eyed Boy*, haven't you?" Her hair fell across her face as she bent to pour another cup of tea.

"Many times," Claire said.

"That book had a powerful effect on people, and one of them was Lou. He read it when it first came out, tracked Jonathan down, and they became friends. More than friends. There's a special relationship between an author and a fan. The fan has found someone to give voice to his thoughts, the author has found a kindred spirit. That was Lou and Jonathan. Lou had no family, and he considered Jonathan his honorary brother. He was in Vietnam in 1966, which is why Jonathan said he was worried about him. We keep in touch. He comes back here from time to time for the Veterans Day ceremony at the Vietnam Memorial in Angel Fire. I'll be interested to hear what *he* thinks of the journal."

"Ada would prefer that no one else saw it."

"Ada Vail has no power over me," Jennie said.

The cat came into the room, jumped onto the sofa, and curled up in her lap. Its color was a perfect complement to Jennie's dress and to the sofa, giving Claire the sensation that Butterscotch was also a part of her costume.

Jennie stroked the cat and said, "Tell me, what did you think of the writing in the journal?"

"I didn't think it was as polished or elegant as *A Blue-Eyed Boy*, but, then, it wasn't written for publication. Who knows what Jonathan would have done with it if . . ."

"If," repeated Jennie, resting her hand on the cat's back. "And what does Ada think?"

"She was more concerned with content than with style."

"She'll want to take out the things she objects to. Money is a loaded gun. Rich people aim their weapon at you and make you dance." Jennie leaned forward suddenly, and the startled cat tumbled out of her lap, hissing and extending its claws as it reached for the floor. "Don't let Ada Vail edit the journal. She'll cut the heart out of it."

"If she holds the rights, we may not have any choice."

"What does Otto think?"

"There's no way of knowing. He doesn't speak since he had the stroke."

"But the eyes react, don't they?"

"You've seen him?"

"Yes, but I haven't been back for a few years. He never was

as rigid as Ada. He might like having Jonathan's journal published as is, but I suppose there's no way for him to tell us that. Curt told me that Tim Sansevera found a duffel bag?" Her husky voice dropped to a whisper, as if she wanted Claire to lean forward to hear better.

Claire, suspecting she was being manipulated, leaned back. "Yes," she said.

"I don't remember there being any duffel bag," Jennie said. "Or a briefcase—Curt said the journal was found in a briefcase. I don't remember that either. We carried everything in backpacks. I could carry a full pack back then, but not anymore. Well, I hope your trip to Slickrock Canyon is productive. As for me, I'll be happy if I never see that place again."

The meeting was over. Jennie stood up and walked Claire to the door.

Continuing north on Route 14, Claire listened to sixties music, thinking it might help her understand Jennie Dell better. She had two tapes that her brother had put together from records he'd found in thrift shops. One tape reflected his taste for the apocalyptic—The Doors, The Rolling Stones, the Beatles' *White Album*. The other was the gentler music that Claire preferred—early Beatles, Cat Stevens, Van Morrison. She played the second tape, and when she heard Fleetwood Mac, she thought about the resemblance Jennie had to the mature Stevie Nicks: the husky voice, the thick blond hair, the skill at manipulating her dress—or was "costume" a better word? She suspected there had also been a resemblance to the young Stevie Nicks, who was known for her wildness and had once made the statement that fast cars, drugs, and money can ruin your life.

She put millions of dollars of cocaine up her nose, but still had one of the best voices in rock. Whatever Jennie had done in the sixties, she seemed to have found a comfortable life now. Unlike Jonathan, Jennie had survived.

When she reached I-25, Claire headed south, turning northwest on Route 44. By the time she got to the red rocks south of Cuba, the tape had played out, and Claire didn't restart it. The beauty here demanded her full attention. It was too overpowering to think or listen to music, so she continued driving in silence. Clouds were gathering when she reached Bloomfield and fires from the oil refineries blazed and flickered like pilot lights against the darkening sky. In Farmington she checked in at a motel. Ten o'clock the next morning was the time Curt had arranged to meet at Slickrock. It allowed him to spend the night at home in Gallup but it meant Claire had to spend the night on the road.

5

Chapter Five

Claire woke up early, had coffee and a doughnut at the motel, and drove the rest of the way to Slickrock Canyon, stopping at the ranger station to get a day permit. As she crossed Cedar Mesa, she was intrigued by the way the trees rippled and blew in the wind like an ocean of green, hiding the mesa's secrets, giving no indication that it was crisscrossed by canyons. Curt had warned her that the turnoff to Slickrock was difficult to find and told her to watch for Mile Marker 23. She kept track of the miles and pulled over when she reached 23. There was no sign for the canyon, but she saw a gate in the barbed-wire fence. She opened the gate, drove through, then got out and closed it behind her. This was BLM land and much of it had been leased for grazing. To leave the gate open was an invitation for cattle to wander onto the highway. The primitive road leading from the gate to the canyon was a bone-rattling combination of ruts, rocks, and sand. Only the dedicated would consider following it very far. Claire didn't see any cattle, but she did see their droppings in the road. She had been down some of the primitive canyon roads in the early morning when marks left in the night were clearly visible in the sand. She'd seen tracks with the chevron pattern of rattlesnake skin and the curving tail prints and tiny footprints of lizards. Dawn was the best time to go into the canyons, and she was annoyed that Curt had arranged the meeting for ten o'clock. Not only had she been forced to spend the night on the road, but starting at ten o'clock gave them fewer daylight hours in the canyon. At least in late October midday wouldn't be unspeakably hot and afternoon thundershowers would be unlikely.

Claire came to a point where the primitive road forked. She didn't know which way to go until she saw that the left fork ended in a grove of cedar trees with shaggy, red bark. There was only one parking spot here, and it had been taken by a white Dodge van with the new-model New Mexico license plate celebrating the balloon festival. Claire liked the colors on this plate, and every time she saw one she was tempted to trade in her old orange-and-yellow Zia sign plate.

She took the right fork, driving until she found a parking space large enough for several cars. Two were already parked here. The red Nissan with the UNM parking sticker had to be Tim's. The government sedan would belong to Curt Devereux. Neither driver was in sight. Was she late? She immediately had the sinking feeling in her stomach that she always got when she was late. She checked her watch and found that, true to form, she was twenty minutes early. She parked her car, picked up her day pack full of trail mix and water, and walked to the edge of the mesa, where she saw the silhouette of a cedar that had been charred by lightning and a pile of stones that had once been an Anasazi lookout tower or storage cist.

The walls of the canyon were the color of sand and burnt sienna, streaked gray in places where minerals had seeped through. Claire could see several hundred feet down into the canyon. Ahead, she could see for miles across the mesa. At a point a mile or so into the canyon, Claire saw two freestanding rocks, several stories high, that had been shaped into sentinels by the elements. In places like this it was easy to understand why people found their destiny in Utah. The hands of the gods appeared everywhere. She knew that petroglyphs were likely to be found near prominent rock formations. The sentinel rocks looked extremely inaccessible to Claire, but the Anasazi favored inaccessible places, where they were protected from intruders.

Slickrock Canyon was a side canyon that led into Grand Gulch, the main canyon, but it had side canyons all its own. Sin Nombre was one, but there were others. Cedar Mesa was a labyrinth of canyons that from the air would resemble a series of question marks. Standing at the edge of Slickrock, Claire found that it became easier to believe that Jonathan Vail could have disappeared without a trace. Looking across the canyon was forbidding, looking down induced vertigo. The ledges were dotted with green brush, but the floor had turned the gold of cottonwoods in October. Claire knew that in the spring wild roses bloomed here. Enough water flowed through the canyons to support life. One could spend a long time on the floor of the canyon, but the Indians had lived in the high caves, and that was where Jonathan's effects had been found. When Claire looked across the canyon she saw markings on the wall—the mineral streaks that resembled rock art and numerous dark spots that could be shadows or caves. How had Tim ever found the right one? Where were Tim and Curt Devereux? What would she do if they didn't show up?

In some of the main canyons the trails were carefully marked by stone cairns, but this wasn't one of them. Slickrock was a primitive canyon, and hikers proceeded at their own peril. The fact that the entrance was unmarked meant that only the most determined would find it. Claire walked along the rim looking for a way in. There were no footprints on the rock to guide her or to indicate where Tim and Curt had gone. They might have entered the canyon, they might be along the rim where there was enough piñon, juniper, and cedar to hide them from view. Pieces of the rim had broken off with geometrical precision and fallen into the canyon. A massive rock lying beneath her had straight edges and a corner that was nearly square, but its surface was softened by the subtle mauve, green, and rust shades of lichen. There was a brushy area between the rock and the canyon wall that was wide enough for a person to squeeze through. It wasn't a path, but it was a way in, possibly the best way. It was not a route that Claire was eager to follow, though—you couldn't see where your feet were going in the weeds, and there were plenty of places for snakes to hide beneath the boulder. She wondered whether rattlesnakes were out at this time of year. She was considering yelling for Tim and Curt when she saw the top of Curt's sunburned head coming around the edge of the squared-off boulder below her.

"Curt," she called.

He looked up and wiped his face with a bandanna. "Excuse me, I was just . . ." His face turned red. "Relieving myself. No place to do that in the slickrock."

He climbed up to the rim, maneuvering between the rock and the wall. He used a walking staff, but otherwise showed no concern for snakes. When he reached Claire, he stopped to catch his breath.

"Have you seen Tim?" she asked.

"No. I woke up at four this morning and couldn't go back to sleep, so I drove on up, stopping at the Navajo Cafe in Bluff for breakfast. I was here by nine. Tim's car was parked, but I haven't seen him. There's an overnight permit from the ranger station on his dashboard, so I'm assuming he camped in the canyon. It's possible he didn't feel like hiking back up again." He glanced at his watch. "I think we ought to go looking for him. I searched the rim and he's not here. There's only one way out of the canyon, so we're sure to pass him if he comes looking for us. We don't have that many hours of daylight. Tim drew me a map giving me a pretty good idea of where he'll be."

"Will we see snakes at this time of year?"

"It's unlikely, but I'll go first. This is actually the worst spot for rattlers. When we get farther down, we'll be walking on slickrock. It's good that you wore hiking boots. They'll help protect you from snakes, and they'll grip well on the rock, too. Did you bring plenty of water?"

"Yes."

"Ready?" Curt asked.

"Ready," said Claire.

He began hiking through the brush, squeezing between the rock and the hard place. Claire followed, trying to keep up a conversation to let any snakes know they were coming, but Curt's back was stiff and his answers were monosyllabic. After a while she gave up. They walked through the brush for fifteen minutes, then came around the side of the boulder and were on the slickrock, which presented another challenge—keeping her balance. There was nothing to hold on to, and Claire had to grip tight with the soles of her feet. It was difficult now, but if it got wet, it would be treacherous. As they got deeper into the canyon, the boulders along the canyon walls took on intriguing shapes. Claire saw an owl looking over its shoulder and a falcon at rest. The sky narrowed. At the floor, only a ribbon of sky would be visible. A storm could blow up without warning, but it was unlikely to rain at this time of year, and the sky Claire could see remained a deep blue. She found this kind of hiking satisfying. Progress was easy to measure, and she didn't have any trouble keeping up with Curt. Tai chi didn't develop climbing muscles, but it did develop attentiveness, which Claire found useful. Soon they came to a place with a pouroff that obviously became a waterfall when it rained. Curt climbed down first and extended his hand to Claire.

In about an hour they were at the floor of the canyon. Curt stopped to drink from his water bottle and Claire joined him. She could hear water trickling inside a cave, indicating that it had rained at some point, and there was an occasional pool in the stream channel that marked the canyon floor. The cotton-woods were smaller here than they were in the Rio Grande Bosque, but they were still magnificent. The leaves danced in the wind, and those that had fallen to the ground rushed underfoot. Claire loved the textured bark of the cottonwoods and the way the branches curved and wandered like a country road.

"Have you seen any sign of Tim?" she asked Curt. There was a natural path beside the stream, but it was too hard to hold a footprint.

"Not here, but the brush up above looked bent, as if someone had been through it recently."

"Could there have been some confusion about where or when we were to meet him?"

"It's possible," Curt replied. Claire couldn't tell if his bland expression came naturally or as practiced from years of working for the federal government. "Tim gave me good directions, but he struck me as an impulsive person."

"Are we near the cave?"

"A couple of miles," Curt said. "It's an easy walk until we get to Sin Nombre. Then we'll have some climbing to do."

"I'd like to try calling him."

"Sure, why not?" Curt shrugged and took another drink from his water bottle.

"Tim," Claire yelled as loud as she could. "Tim!" The sound echoed around the canyon and came back "Tim, Tim, Tim, Tim" in ever descending notes. Eventually the echo died out with no response, leaving Claire feeling foolish.

"Ready?" Curt asked, putting his water bottle back in his day pack.

"Ready," she replied.

He continued walking beside the stream channel and Claire followed. She had thought the time spent hiking might loosen him up, but he looked as stiff now as he had when they started out. It was nearly noon, and the sun was shining into the canyon, casting shadows beneath their feet. Claire could easily keep up with Curt's steady, deliberate pace. The air was cool, clear, and energizing. The more she walked, the stronger she felt.

They continued in silence for a mile or so before Curt stopped again. "That's Sin Nombre Canyon," he said, pointing west with his walking staff.

Claire had been watching the ground and could have easily missed the turnoff. The bottom of Sin Nombre Canyon was thick with brush and boulders, but when she looked up, the walls of the side canyon were clear. It was a smaller, narrower version of Slickrock—buff and burnt sienna sandstone streaked dark by minerals; a mixture of ledge, rock slides, and indentations in the walls.

"Sin Nombre is full of boulders, and it's easy to get lost in here, so you don't want to lose sight of me. If I start going too fast, you let me know," Curt said.

"All right," Claire replied.

Water rushed through this narrow canyon with considerable force, scattering boulders like pebbles. Going over or around them, a form of climbing known as boulder hopping, was a challenge that kept Claire focused. There was no sign that humans had ever been here, yet Claire knew that Anasazi had lived in Sin Nombre and that people had climbed all over it looking for some trace of Jonathan Vail. One of those people was Tim Sansevera, whose absence was casting a pall over her day like a cloud obscuring the sun. Was it due to impulsiveness, error, or something else? The only way to find out was to continue.

After they had climbed for forty-five minutes, Curt stopped for another water break. To Claire, he appeared to be showing a little more excitement as he closed in on their goal. His back seemed less stiff. His eyes were brighter. He finished his drink, put the cap back on the bottle, and pointed to a spot on the canyon wall high up near the rim. "See that?" he asked. "It's a half-moon petroglyph."

Claire could see something on the canyon wall, but she couldn't identify it as a half-moon or anything else.

"Here." Curt took a pair of binoculars from his backpack.

She fiddled with the adjustment on the binoculars until she could make out the half-moon.

"Now look to the right of it," Curt said. "You'll see the entrance to the cave where Tim claims he found the journal."

Claire moved the binoculars over a rock slide until she came to a small, rounded opening shaped like an *horno*.

"How do we get there?"

"That's for Tim to show us."

"Wouldn't it have been easier to climb down from the mesa?" Claire asked.

"Easier to climb down, but harder to find. I didn't have a compass reading. There are no landmarks to follow on Cedar Mesa, and it can be difficult to find your way. The trees all look the same. I think that overhang up ahead is a good place to begin the climb. It's also the best campsite in the canyon. It's got a southern exposure. It's got a spring. I'm hoping Tim will be there or will have left some indication of where he went." Curt's face turned red again. "Excuse me. I, um . . . have to, um, relieve myself again. Too much coffee this morning."

"I'll meet you at the overhang," Claire said.

Curt stepped around a boulder. Claire heard branches rustle, a canyon wren call, and then silence. She continued uphill, climbing over a boulder that was as tall as she was. Once the boulder was behind her, her only points of reference were the canyon rim, the half-moon petroglyph, and the overhang, a slab of rock that was clearly in sight ahead. From this spot there was no way of telling where Curt had gone. She climbed a little farther, then saw something that resembled a blue tarp beneath the overhang. As she got closer, she realized it was a tent, an encouraging sign that Tim had camped here. Had Curt gotten the plans mixed up? Had Tim intended to meet them here all along?

She called to him, but once again there was no answer. This time she hadn't yelled loud enough to cause an avalanche of echoes. She walked to the overhang, saw the tent and a camp stove. She looked inside the tent and found a sleeping bag and a paperback copy of *A Blue-Eyed Boy*, but nothing else. The soil here was sandy, and there were footprints of running shoes somewhat larger than Claire's leading toward the canyon wall. The footprints disappeared where the slickrock began, but

Claire continued in their direction and saw a way to climb the canyon wall negotiating natural stairways from ledge to ledge. A raven flew over and cawed twice. Something rustled in the underbrush. There was a rotten smell—a dead animal or spoiled food. Claire climbed to the top of the overhang, felt the warmth of the sun, heard the sound of flies buzzing, and came across a body lying on top of the slickrock. It was grotesquely swollen, smashed and bloody as if it had fallen from a great height.

"Oh, God!" she cried. This bloody mess couldn't be Tim— yet the head, skewed sideways by the fall, had his reddish-brown ponytail. How do flies find destruction so quickly? she thought absurdly as she knelt to feel for a pulse. There was none. "Tim," she whispered, and then she began to yell for Curt, screaming until her throat was raw. She heard some sort of response, but she couldn't tell who or what it was or if it was an echo. The stench became unbearable. She poured some water on her bandanna and pressed it to her face. Footsteps pounded the slickrock, and Curt was beside her, red-faced and struggling to catch his breath.

"He must have fallen from a ledge," he said. "Is he dead?"

"Yes."

"I'll radio the ranger station for help."

While Curt got on his radio, Claire mentally compared the pattern on the soles of Tim's running shoes to the footprints she'd seen and found a match. She looked up toward the canyon rim where a vulture had become a warning in the sky. It would have been easy enough for Tim to have fallen while climbing up to the cave or coming back down. Why hadn't he waited for them? When had he fallen?

He had landed on his back, with his backpack beneath him. If there were any clues to be found in the backpack, they were inaccessible. His green eyes were wide open, frozen in a fixed and terrifying stare. She wished there were some way of knowing what images were recorded on the retina, what last sights Tim had seen.

"The BLM will send a helicopter to take the body out," Curt said.

"How long will that take?"

"An hour. It's stopping to pick up Ellen Frank and Ray Vigil at the ranger station."

The thought of sitting here for an hour with Tim's blank, staring eyes was deeply disturbing. "Would you mind if I closed his eyes?" she asked Curt.

"Go ahead," Curt replied. "I'll spread out his tent to make it easier for the helicopter to find us."

He walked away, leaving Claire alone with Tim. Curt hadn't said so, but she knew someone needed to stay with the body. Another vulture had joined the first in a leisurely gyre. Claire found it easier to look at Tim once his eyes were closed.

Now that the initial shock was over, the tragedy of his death was beginning to sink in. Tim had a passion for life and for his work and a promising future. This would be a terrible loss for the family and friends who knew him well and loved him. Claire's heart went out to them, especially his mother. Claire herself had a son who was close to Tim's age. The pain she would feel if she lost her own son was beyond comprehension. She made up her mind to track down Tim's mother and tell her what she knew of her son. She would tell her of finding Tim here but there were things she wouldn't repeat—the flies, the vultures, the blood, the shattered limbs, the stench.

She had turned her back to the body and fallen into a slump, oppressed by thoughts of Tim and his family. Now she glanced up and saw that the vultures were moving into the canyon—

perhaps thinking that she had died, too. She stood up, yelled, and flapped her arms, sending the vultures higher. While she was on her feet she could see that Curt had spread the tent over the boulders so it formed a blue rectangle in the middle of the canyon, easy to spot from the air. At least no time would be wasted searching for them.

She wondered what Curt would do with *A Blue-Eyed Boy*, whether it would be considered evidence, whether Tim's death would be treated as an accident or a crime. He had died very close to where his hero had disappeared. Was that merely a bitter irony or something more sinister? He could have met somebody here. The only footprints Claire saw in the sand appeared to be his, but there were other ways to get onto the ledges and into the canyon. There was the white van in the parking lot. And there was Curt, who had been coming out of the canyon as Claire arrived, who was nowhere in sight when she found the body. She thought back to her conversation with Tim. As she recalled, he hadn't told her exactly when he was meeting Curt.

When she stood up, the flies had backed off, but now that she had settled into thought again, they resumed their buzzing. She thought it seemed to be getting louder, but then she realized the buzzing was blending into the sound of the helicopter. She looked up, saw the chopper come over the far canyon and cross to this side. The helicopter sound stopped, and Claire assumed it had landed somewhere on the rim, although she couldn't see it.

Curt climbed back onto the overhang, wiping his face with his bandanna. "The rangers will hike down," he said. "The helicopter is going to lower a sling and the rangers will load Tim's body onto it. The helicopter can pull you out, or you can climb up to the mesa with me and get a ride back."

The thought of dangling from a rope in the confines of Sin Nombre Canyon didn't appeal to Claire. "I'll climb," she said.

"It's five hundred feet."

"I can handle it."

The rangers began descending the canyon wall. To Claire they looked as quick and agile as mountain goats leaping from ledge to ledge. When they reached the bottom, they shook Curt's hand and introduced themselves to Claire as Ellen Frank and Ray Vigil. Ellen remembered that Claire had called the ranger station after Tim turned in the journal. She was a medium-sized, deeply tanned woman with a stocky build. Her hair was brown and chopped off just below her chin. Her agility led Claire to place her age at forty or less, although her skin showed the wrinkles of an older woman. Ray Vigil was about the same height. His dark hair was cut in bangs that formed a fringe beneath his ranger hat. Claire's impression was that he was a few years younger than Ellen. That impression was reinforced when Ellen took charge, bending to examine Tim's body.

"It looks like he fell from a ledge. High up, I'd say."

"Could he have fallen yesterday or last night?" Claire asked.

"I doubt it," Ellen said. "There are predators in the canyons who would have found their way to a body in the night. The medical examiner will do an autopsy and give us an approximate time of death."

"Did it rain last night?"

"No. It hasn't rained here for several days."

"When you climbed down did you see any sign that anyone else had been here?"

"No," Ray said.

"We'll examine the canyon thoroughly before we leave," Ellen said. "This is the student who found Jonathan Vail's journal, correct?"

"Right," answered Claire.

"Do you know where exactly?"

"A cave just to the west of the half-moon petroglyph," Curt said.

"We may not be able to get there until tomorrow. Would you take a look on your way out?" Ellen asked Curt, making it clear that she was in charge of this investigation and causing Claire to wonder if she intended to take charge of the thirty-year-old investigation as well. At this point, Claire hoped she would.

"Will do," said Curt in a noncommittal tone.

"Any questions?" Ellen asked him.

"No," he answered, once again showing a noticeable lack of curiosity for an investigator.

"Are you comfortable with hiking out?" Ellen asked Claire.

"Yes," Claire said.

"I'd like to talk to you when you return to Albuquerque. No telling when we'll get done here. Could you meet me at the ranger station tomorrow morning? Say nine o'clock?"

"I'll be there."

"Let's get going," Ellen said, turning to Ray Vigil and dismissing Curt and Claire.

Ray got on his radio and spoke to the helicopter pilot. Curt hoisted his pack and started to climb. Claire followed. "Less than a year left," she wanted to commiserate with him. They had been through a harrowing experience together and she felt a bond, but Curt's stiff back seemed impervious to insult, indifferent to kindness. Some people believed that hiking down was harder than hiking up because of the strain that braking put on the knee muscles. Hiking up was just a matter of putting one foot in front of the other slow enough that one didn't run out of breath.

Claire heard the helicopter and stopped to watch it lower the sling down to the rangers. Curt didn't even turn around. He just kept on hiking. Once the body was carried out, Claire would be relieved, knowing that Tim would eventually be returned to his mother. She resumed hiking slowly, searching the rocks for anything that might explain Tim's death. The climbing was slow, but it wasn't treacherous. The ledges were wide and flat, and there were natural steps between them.

Eventually Curt stopped to drink from his water bottle and waited for her to catch up. Claire drank from her own bottle, careful not to look back down into the canyon. By now they were nearing the rim. The drop was close to five hundred feet and precipitous. When they reached the petroglyph, she saw that it was, indeed, a half-moon. She couldn't remember ever seeing a half-moon petroglyph before, but this one appeared old enough to be authentic. She imagined the hands that placed it on the wall several hundred years ago. From here the going got more difficult. The rock slide between the petroglyph and the cave had the potential to roll and slip underfoot. It would be a lethal place to lose one's balance.

"I'd say this is where Sansevera got into trouble," Curt said. "It's a straight trajectory from this spot to where he landed. He never should have come here alone."

"He did it before," Claire replied.

"So he said. I intend to examine the cave, but no need for you to come if you're uncomfortable."

"I want to see it," Claire replied. She couldn't get this close to the Jonathan Vail mystery and just walk away. And now the mystery of Tim Sansevera had been added to the mystery of Jonathan Vail, two young ghosts to haunt the canyons.

"All right, then. I'll go first," Curt said.

There were no footprints visible in the rock slide, which

might be an indication that Tim hadn't entered it, or that the slide was too fluid to hold a print. Curt kept his backpack on. Claire watched as he put each foot down, but she didn't see much slippage. When he reached the ledge on the far side of the slide, he turned and tossed her the end of a piece of rope. Claire couldn't quite reach it, so she took her first tentative steps without Curt's support. She had taken off her backpack, and put it on the ledge before starting out, thinking that would help her maintain her balance. The slide felt loose, but she had the sense of solid ground underneath. She extended her arms and spread her fingers for equilibrium, slowly taking one step, then another. On the third step—just as Curt's rope was almost within reach—her foot dislodged a rock the size of a fist. She watched helplessly as it rolled to the edge of the ledge, balanced briefly, and tumbled off.

"Oh, no," Claire cried, wondering if she should warn the rangers, if they could even hear her. The rock created its own warning system as it bounced off the canyon walls, crashing from ledge to ledge, seemingly getting larger and louder as it descended into the canyon, dislodging other rocks and gathering them into its fall. It seemed to take forever before the avalanche crashed onto the canyon floor, sending up a cloud of dust and raising a cacophony of echoes that resembled a flock of screaming ravens. Claire stared at the dust with the panicky feeling she got when she was too close to the heights or depths.

She turned her attention back to the ledge, wishing there was a rail between her and the dropoff, something to break the line of vision, something to hold on to. She took one more step, bent down and picked up the rope, although she would have preferred to negotiate without it. She didn't want her balance to depend on Curt Devereux. If he let go of the rope, she would take the same path the rock had taken.

"Two more steps, and you'll be all right," Curt said.

Claire was relieved to put her foot down on the ledge, which was several feet wide and felt solid as a bridge. The entrance to the cave was ten feet away. It was littered with rock debris about four feet high and shaped like a beehive or an *horno*. As Claire let go of the rope her hands trembled in relief and excitement.

"This means a lot to you, doesn't it?" Curt asked.

"A lot."

"You go first."

He backed against the canyon wall. She squeezed past him, bent down, climbed over the rocks that had once concealed the entrance, and entered the low opening into the cave. Her first sensation was of coolness and darkness. In the time it took for her eyes to adjust, she imagined what she might see. All she could reasonably expect was a duffel bag, but the image in her mind was of Jonathan Vail sitting by a fire writing in his journal. Once her eyes made the adjustment she explored the cave visually, not wanting to step inside any farther and cause any damage. It was about fifteen feet deep, the top was curved, the floor, which was Slickrock, was so clean it might have been swept. No animal or human track was visible. There were no implements, there was no duffel bag, no sign that a human had ever been here. It was absolutely, totally empty and a crushing disappointment for Claire, who felt like all the rock in the cave weighed her down. Something blocked the light. She turned and saw Curt crawling through the entrance.

"Are you sure this is the right place?" she asked.

"Tim described it as the cave just beyond the rockslide to the west of the half-moon petroglyph. It has to be this one." He dropped his pack, took out a flashlight and began circling the sides of the cave, shining the light into every nook and cranny. It was big enough to hide out in, but too close to the abyss for

Claire to ever consider it. She would never be able to forget that just beyond the mouth of this cave was a five-hundred-foot dropoff. It made it safe from intruders but not from the siren song of acrophobia that whispered to anyone foolish enough to listen, you can jump, you can fly. She wondered how much time Jonathan had spent in this cave, whether Jennie had ever been here.

"There's no duffel bag," she said.

"No," Curt replied, "but look at this." He beamed his light beside a rock at the rear of the cave.

Claire still did not want to step any farther inside. She craned her neck and saw, carved into the rock wall, the initials JV. Jonathan Vail—but had they been carved by him or by an imitator?

"A BLM archaeologist should be able to date and authenticate that," Curt said.

Sunlight shimmered through the entry. When Claire looked out, all she could see was the dust they had stirred up. Had there ever been a duffel bag? Had Tim told the truth? Had Jennie? Would everything connected to Jonathan Vail end in illusion and dust?

Curt completed his search and came up with nothing else. Claire imagined that Ellen Frank and Ray Vigil would search, too, but it was unlikely they would find anything either. She and Curt hiked up to the mesa, where the helicopter waited. The plan was for the pilot to fly them out, then come back for Tim's body. It was a fairly easy climb from the cave and Claire thought it would have been better to have brought the duffel bag out across the mesa than through the canyon—if one knew the way, if there really was a duffel bag.

Claire looked back into the canyon from the window of the helicopter. There was no sign of the rangers or the blue tent among the boulders on the floor of Sin Nombre. The motion of the helicopter made the canyon walls shimmer, reminding Claire of Jonathan's comparison to La Sagrada Familia. She looked for the white van as they flew over the parking area, but didn't see it.

The helicopter dropped her and Curt on the flat rim of Slickrock Canyon, and they walked back to their vehicles. Tim's tiny red car was a sad reminder of all that had happened.

"The rangers should take the keys from Tim so they can drive his car out," Claire said.

"I'm sure they'll think of that," Curt replied in a soothing voice. "You're staying till tomorrow?"

"Yes. I'll find a motel in Blanding and talk to Ellen Frank in the morning. And you?"

"I'm going to spend the night in Bluff and take a look around tomorrow. It's been a tough day."

"It has," Claire said.

Curt poked the ground with the toe of his hiking boot. "I'm very sorry it turned out this way."

"I feel terrible for Tim and his family."

Curt shook her hand. "Keep in touch," he said.

"You, too," she replied.

Claire was exhausted by the time she got to Blanding. She found a room at the Prospector Motel with knotty pine paneling and a pink chenille spread, which she found comforting. She ran a hot bath, climbed in, and lay there for an hour trying to soak away the sweat, the dirt, the stench, the flies, the blood, the horror of the day. She got into bed and pulled up the chenille spread, prepared for a sleepless night. To her surprise she fell into a deep sleep and didn't wake until dawn. She packed up, had a cup of coffee in the motel office, and drove to the ranger station for her appointment with Ellen Frank.

6

Chapter Six

It was early enough that Claire could feel the coolness and the moisture left over from the night as she drove to the ranger station. In this remote corner of Utah, every morning bore a resemblance to the first morning, but that morning would have filled any observer with awe and this one filled her with despair. The shock of Tim's death had passed, the emotional Novocain had worn off, and her heart ached. She drove through Butler Wash and across Comb Ridge, where the sandstone was arrested in the angle of repose, the angle that a dune reaches just before falling over. The ridge was a bulge in the earth's crust that extended for eighty miles. To Claire it resembled a series of dunes stretching into infinity. It was a landscape that always seemed to be in motion, soothing to look at but unforgiving of human error.

Claire knew that rangers often saw the results of human error—people wandering off without a map, wearing the wrong shoes, carrying insufficient water, unaware of approaching thunderstorms. Mistakes very quickly turned into disasters. She wondered if Tim's death would be treated as one more example of human carelessness. It had all the ingredients of an impulsive young man climbing a canyon wall apparently alone.

She parked her car in the visitors lot and went into the trailer that served as the ranger station, giving her name to a volunteer who manned the desk. While she waited for Ellen Frank, she took a look at a selection of books for sale. Along with books about the flora and fauna of the area, she saw the original journal and *A Blue-Eyed Boy*.

Ellen Frank appeared and led her down the hall to her office. She was a few inches shorter than Claire, but her confident attitude made her seem taller. Her office was small and tidy, with a window that looked out on a juniper bush.

"Coffee?" she asked.

"No thanks."

"Did you spend the night in Blanding?"

"Yes."

"I hope you got a good night's sleep." Ellen sat down and motioned for Claire to do the same.

"Better than I expected."

Ellen looked wide awake and fully prepared. Her uniform was crisp. Every hair was in place. Her teeth were so even they appeared to have been filed. She wasn't someone Claire would want to confront if she hadn't had any sleep.

"Tell me what you know about Tim Sansevera," Ellen said, leaning forward and putting her elbows on her desk.

"He was a grad student who was writing his dissertation on

Jonathan Vail. I'm in charge of the Vail archives. I gave him access to the papers, so when he found the journal in the cave, he brought it to me. He was very excited to have found it."

"And you believe the journal is authentic?"

"I do. It has also been read by Jonathan's mother and by Jennie Dell, and they believe it to be authentic, too. The library intends to have it verified by an expert."

"Jennie Dell is the woman who was with Vail in Slickrock Canyon, right?"

"Right."

"How did she get the journal?"

"Curt Devereux gave her a copy."

"Ah," said Ellen. She picked up a pencil and rolled it between her fingers. "Tell me about the duffel bag."

"Tim told me he saw a duffel bag in the cave where he found the journal, but he was carrying too much to bring it out."

"Did he say what was in it?"

"Clothes."

"So the plan was that you, Curt, and Tim were to meet at the trailhead to Slickrock Canyon at ten yesterday and look for the duffel bag?" The brightness of Ellen's amber eyes made Claire feel she was under a spotlight. She had to remind herself that she hadn't done anything stupid or wrong.

"Trailhead" struck her as a misnomer, since there hadn't actually been any trail in Slickrock Canyon. She chose her words carefully. "That was the arrangement Curt and I had. You'll have to ask him what arrangement he made with Tim. When I got to the parking lot, I saw Tim's and Curt's vehicles. In the left fork I also saw a white Dodge van with New Mexico plates. No one was there. I walked around the ledge for a while looking for Tim and Curt, then I saw Curt climbing out of the canyon. He said he'd gone there to relieve himself."

"Did you get the license plate number of the van by any chance?"

"No. It was the New Mexico balloon plate. That's all I noticed. It seemed like an older model, so it was unlikely to be a rental."

"I didn't see any van when we flew over in the helicopter. We'll check to see if we gave a permit to a New Mexico van recently. We might be able to track the owner down. We try to register people who enter the canyons. One reason is that it makes it easier for us to find them when they get into trouble. But it's a huge area, and we can't police all of it. People enter the canyons and camp without registering. It's an honor system. We did issue Tim a permit to camp in Sin Nombre Friday night."

"If you had a suspect in Tim's death, could you check motor vehicle records to see if that person owned a Dodge van?"

"We could." Ellen paused and fingered her pencil. "*If* there is a suspect. First we have to determine the cause of death. We'll continue our investigation while we're waiting for the autopsy to come back."

"If you should find evidence that Tim's death wasn't accidental, what would you do?"

"Turn it over to local law enforcement and the FBI. We're not equipped to handle a murder investigation here."

"Will Curt remain in charge of the Vail investigation?"

"Most likely. He has seniority, and he worked on it before."

"Did you notify Tim's family of his death?"

"Yes. I tracked down his mother in Albuquerque." Ellen stared out her window into the branches of the juniper. "She was very upset of course."

Claire could well imagine. "Would you mind giving me her name and number? I'd like to call her when I get back to town."

Ellen wrote down the information and handed it to Claire.

"When exactly did Tim say that he found the duffel bag?" she asked.

"Last Sunday, a week ago. He brought the journal to me on Monday. That's when I reported the find to you and to Curt."

"By now someone else could have come across it and taken it. It should have been reported to us, but there's no guarantee it would be. We might have gone looking for it ourselves, except that Curt asked to do it and he did it on his own time. People still come to me with theories about what happened to Jonathan Vail. There's an amazing amount of interest in someone who disappeared in 1966. I've always wondered why."

It was Claire's job to keep the memory of Jonathan Vail alive, and his enduring legend was a subject to which she had given considerable thought. "He wrote a book that influenced a lot of people, he disappeared at a young age, and the mystery of his disappearance has never been solved. It's a puzzle that keeps people interested."

"I hear the same theories over and over again. Vail is still alive, there's a child somewhere, he's hiding out and dodging the draft on the Navajo reservation. I know that one isn't true. If Jonathan were on the reservation, someone would have reported it by now. Besides, draft dodgers got amnesty years ago. Sam Ogelthorpe, who owns the Comb Ranch, talks to me about it occasionally. He claims he saw Jonathan killing a cow on his ranch two days before he was reported missing. But it was night, it was raining, Sam hated hippies. Who knows what he saw? Maybe it was an apparition, maybe it was a mountain lion, maybe it was another hungry hippie. Whatever it was left a dead cow, but any footprints washed away in the rain."

"Is Sam still alive?"

"Oh, yeah. Still ranching, still grazing on BLM land. Even though Sam has nothing but contempt for Jonathan Vail, I guess the connection makes him feel important, like he's a part of history somehow. Is that what it's all about?"

"That's part of it." Claire was reluctant to bring up the next subject, but Ellen had given her an opening. "There is also the theory that Curt didn't conduct a thorough investigation, that he was blinded by his attraction to Jennie Dell."

Ellen smiled with precision. "I've heard that one, too," she said. Her smile disappeared, and her face went bureaucratically blank, almost as blank as Curt's, although she'd had less experience in cultivating the expression. "To be fair to Curt, this area was very primitive in the sixties, and he had limited resources. It's quite possible that Jonathan Vail and Tim Sansevera both died by falling off a ledge. Maybe even, by a strange coincidence, the same ledge. We were lucky enough to find Tim. Jonathan's bones could have washed into the San Juan, or they could remain in Sin Nombre Canyon. They might still be found. Every time we get a hard rain the boulders shift and the configuration of the canyon changes. One day one of those changes may expose Vail's bones. Bones are a good witness. They don't lie, and they never forget."

"It's possible for the cave to have closed and opened up again?"

"Absolutely."

"Could Curt and I have gone into the wrong cave?"

"That's also possible. We'll look into the others while we're conducting our investigation. If we find any artifacts of Jonathan Vail, they'll get passed on to Curt. Are you going home today?"

"Yes," Claire said.

Ellen stood up and gave Claire a firm handshake. "Have a good trip. I appreciate your help."

Claire drove south on Highway 261, planning to drive down the Moki Dugway and stop in Bluff for lunch. Route 261 paralleled Comb Ridge, which looked more like cresting waves to her now than dunes. She thought of grief as an ocean that came at the grieving person in waves—submerging, receding, submerging again. She could imagine that Tim's mother would feel she was drowning in grief.

She came to a dirt road with a rusty sign that read COMB RANCH. On a whim, Claire turned in. It was a long drive across the mesa, on a road so rough it made her truck sound like a bucket of bolts and buck like an ornery horse. It was a test of the effectiveness of her shock absorbers, and they seemed to be failing. The road was so bad there were points at which she considered turning around, but Sam Ogelthorpe was another character in the Jonathan Vail mystery, someone she had wondered about for years, and she couldn't pass up the opportunity to meet him.

Eventually the road ended at a ramshackle ranch house and outbuildings. This was a hardscrabble working ranch, not the hobby of a wealthy absentee owner. A pack of dogs snoozed in the yard and on the porch. They raised their heads as Claire parked her pickup, but didn't bother to bark. When a man came out the front door and walked over to her, the dogs stood up and followed. He wore jeans, boots, and a black cowboy hat with a dip in the brim that hid the upper portion of his face. The lower part wore a shaggy white mustache.

Claire climbed out of her truck, and the rancher extended his hand. "Howdy," he said. "I'm Sam Ogelthorpe." He'd been ranching here thirty years ago, so he wasn't a young man, but it was hard to pinpoint his age. He could have been anywhere from fifty-five to seventy-five. Although his hair was white, he didn't have the slow movements of an old man. His face was weathered, but out here that could happen at a young age. Claire knew that if ranchers didn't get killed by accidents, they tended to live a long time. In some ways it was a very healthy life.

"Good to meet you," she said. "My name is Claire Reynier. I'm the archivist for the Jonathan Vail papers at the University of New Mexico."

"Well, damn," said Sam. "I was wondering if you people would ever show up."

"Excuse me?"

"You ought to put my name in your archives right along with Vail's. I may not be the last person to see him in Utah, but I'm the last person who's willing to admit it."

Everyone liked to have their place in history, Claire thought, however small. "Of course you're in our archives," she reassured him. "I've been wanting to meet you for a long time. If you ever get to the university, I'd be glad to show you the archives."

Harrison soothed the wealthy donors, and Claire got the cowboys, which was all right with her; cowboys were less predictable than rich people. The stroking was deliberate, and it appeared to work. Sam's crustiness fell away like mud dropping off a dried-up boot.

"I may just do that," he replied.

"I hope you will," said Claire.

"What brings you to Comb Ranch?"

"A student discovered Jonathan Vail's missing journal in a cave in Sin Nombre Canyon last week. I went back with Curt Devereux to see if there might be anything else in the cave, and we found the student dead."

"How'd that happen?"

"It looks like he fell off a ledge. Ellen Frank is investigating."

"Easy enough to fall in the canyons," Sam replied. "Ellen's

smart. She'll find out what happened—unlike Curt Devereux, who couldn't find his way out of a paper bag. Vail was on my property in 1966. Devereux came over and looked at the spot, but that's all he ever did. I can show you exactly where I saw Vail if you're interested. It'd be somethin' to tell your students about."

"I'd like that," Claire replied.

"My truck's out back."

"Let's take mine," Claire said. "The keys are in the ignition." She hoped that would keep Sam from bringing the dogs who were a scruffy mixture of hound and mutt, saliva and fleas, dander and dirt. People drove around with dogs in the back of their pickups all the time, but she wasn't comfortable doing it. If you braked too hard, the dog became an unguided missile.

Sam ordered the dogs to stay put, got in her truck, and directed her down a ranch road that was even worse than his access road. It was basically two ruts, and it took all her concentration to keep the Chevy's wheels in the track.

"Do you mind if I smoke?" Sam asked.

Claire did mind, but they were on his property, so she said, "No" and rolled down her window. Sam did the same, resting his right arm on the open window between puffs. It felt like they'd gone as far north as Slickrock Canyon, but it was actually only a few miles before Sam told her to stop.

They got out of the truck, and Claire followed him across the mesa, noticing his worn boots and rolling cowboy walk. It soon became clear how hard it could be to find one's way among the piñon, cedar, and juniper. They were all approximately the same size, color, and shape, making it nearly impossible to distinguish one tree from another. The land was flat and dry, so there were no changes in elevation or water channels for guidance. It didn't take long for the trees to close in behind them, concealing

Claire's truck. There were no landmarks to indicate where they were going or where they had been. Even Comb Ridge was not reliable. The peaks were so identical, Claire could look away for a second and not be able to tell which ridge she had previously focused on. You were left to navigate by the stars, the sun, or a compass, if you had one. The dogs would have been a help; dogs can always find their way back.

Sam walked ahead, squinting at the ground. He wasn't wearing glasses, and Claire wondered how well he could see. He was old enough for corrective lenses. Why wasn't he wearing them? Stubbornness seemed a more likely cause than vanity. There was no visible trail, and she looked down at the ground wondering what guided him. Every now and then she saw an unfiltered cigarette butt, and she began to feel they were Hansel and Gretel following paper crumbs through the forest.

Sam stopped, dropped the cigarette he'd been smoking and crushed it out with the heel of his cowboy boot. "That's where I saw Vail, by that cedar over there," he said. "Kneeling over the cow he'd killed. He didn't think there was anybody around to notice, I guess."

"What time of day was it?"

"Afternoon, but to him it was dinnertime."

"I understand it was raining that day."

"It was what the Navajos call a female rain, slow and gentle and steady. I could see him all night."

"What did you do?"

"I yelled and he ran away. The guy was a draft dodger and a coward. I was on foot and more interested in protecting my cattle than in chasing him."

"What did he look like?" Claire asked, wondering if Curt had asked the very same questions. Sam seemed more than happy to answer.

"Like a hippie. He was dirty. He had long hair."

"A lot of people looked like that in 1966," Claire reminded him.

"Not on Cedar Mesa they didn't."

"How do you think he got here?"

"He hiked. It's twenty miles from Slickrock as the crow flies. He could have done it in a day. There are no major canyons between here and there. Any jackass with a compass could have found his way to my cattle."

"You didn't have any cattle between here and there?"

"Not then I didn't."

"He wasn't reported missing until two days after you saw him."

Sam watched Claire from under the shadow of his black hat. "The girlfriend didn't know he was missing, or else she was giving him time to get away. After I interrupted his feast, Vail walked out to the highway and got a ride to Mexico."

"If he was a draft dodger, wouldn't he have come back when amnesty was granted?"

"If he was alive, he would have, but anything could have happened to him down there."

"Were you in Vietnam?" Claire asked. If he were at the younger end of her age guesstimate, he could have served in the war.

"They wouldn't take me," Sam replied. "I was too old, but I would have enlisted if I could have. It was a chance to participate in a historical event."

"Do you come out here often?"

"Not nearly as often as I used to. Interest in Vail has faded. Sometimes nowadays I just come out by myself."

"Why?" she asked.

"To keep the trail fresh and the memory alive," Sam said.

"Seen enough?"

"Yes," Claire replied.

While they walked back to the truck in silence Claire wondered why the sighting of someone thirty years ago had remained so important to him. Did he like the attention and the feeling that he had a place in history? Or could it be something more sinister? A persistent rumor among Vail scholars was that after Jonathan killed the cow, Sam shot him and concealed the body. A rancher would know how to use a rifle. Sam might have vision problems now, but that didn't mean he'd had them thirty years ago. Today if a rancher found an animal he didn't like on his property, the expression "shoot, shovel, and shut up" was used to describe the outcome. It was a phrase Claire hadn't heard in 1966, but the impulse was probably the same. She rather liked Sam and didn't want to think he was capable of murder, but thirty years ago he was another person. He might not have known it was a human that was killing his cattle at a distance in the rain. But if he had killed Jonathan Vail or anyone else at that tree, why bring people out to look at the spot? The tree could be a decoy, Claire thought. The victim might have been killed and buried somewhere else on the ranch. It was a place a body could easily be buried and never be found until Sam wanted it to be, which wasn't likely, unless he arranged for it to happen after his death. Anyone with an eye on the past knows that a villain's place in history is assured.

They reached the truck and drove back to the ranch house with Sam smoking and resting his arm on the open window and Claire feeling guilty about the thoughts she'd had. Even so, when they got back to the house and the dogs ran out to greet him, she asked him if they were hunting dogs.

"They're good for nothin' now," Sam replied, "but I used to hunt with 'em."

"What did you hunt?" she asked.

"Cougar."

Mountain lions were hunted with dogs, which pursued them until they climbed a tree, then the hunters shot them down, a pastime Claire didn't consider particularly sporting.

"What does it say about me in your archives?" Sam asked, squinting as if Claire had gotten between him and the sun.

"That you claimed you saw Jonathan Vail kill one of your cows two days before his disappearance was reported to the authorities."

"That's the way it happened," Sam replied. "Sorry to hear about your student. Next time you get out this way, you come back and see me."

"I'd like that," Claire replied.

She left Sam with his memories and his dogs and drove south on Route 261 through the Moki Dugway, where the road dropped fifteen hundred feet by curving down the cliff like a coiled snake. There were no guardrails, and the dropoffs were precipitous. Negotiating the curves took all of Claire's attention, but right before she began the descent she looked out over the Valley of the Gods. The red rock spires of Monument Valley shimmered twenty miles away. The patterns of the cliffs in the near distance resembled a Navajo rug. Behind them, patches of river were visible in the gooseneck section of the San Juan. It was a landscape that inspired awe and doubt.

Once she reached the bottom of the Dugway and a flat stretch of road, Claire inserted her brother's apocalyptic sixties tape. She had often felt like a bystander in those days. She was a student at the University of Arizona and opposed to the war, but unlike Jonathan and Jennie, she had never participated in a demonstration. At the height of the conflict she'd spent six months in Europe, five of them traveling with her Italian boyfriend. She had been separated from the war more by reserve than distance, but she had always wondered if the demonstrators had experienced life more intensely than she did. There was no doubt the soldiers had. She knew men who had never recovered from the war, but she also knew men who had served in Vietnam, come back, and carried on normal lives as scholars, engineers, computer programmers. They might well have killed people, but she never heard them talk about it. It was impossible to tell from her brief encounter with Sam Ogelthorpe whether he was capable of murder. Her instinct said he wasn't, but that was also what she wanted to believe. If Sam was guilty of anything it could be the same things she herself felt guilty of—an overactive imagination, a desire to get close to defining events, a bystander's regret.

When Claire got to Bluff, she didn't stop but kept on driving until the tape played out. By then she was in Farmington. She stopped and got a Lota Burger with green chile and seasoned fries, sat outside at a little table under a red umbrella, and thought about "The Eve of Destruction," "Riders on the Storm," and all the other turbulent music she had just heard. It was the music of close places, chaos, crowds, danger. Remote from the wide-open spaces of this area, but like them in the threat of danger. Jonathan Vail had chosen to retreat to a dangerous place. Tim Sansevera had followed. Curt Devereux and Ellen Frank were from different eras and, at the moment, in charge of different investigations. If there was a link between the two deaths, Claire wondered who would be the one to find it.

7

Chapter Seven

Claire always found it hard to return from the wilderness to the city, from solitude to traffic congestion, from oceans of space to a tiny office, but the beauty of Zimmerman library made the transition easier. The thick walls kept her feeling connected to the earth. The vigas and corbels in the high ceilings of the reading rooms seemed to stretch to infinity. When she opened the door to the center Monday morning, she felt glad to be back, although she wasn't looking forward to the job that lay ahead of her. She had returned from afar with a message of death, and the messenger is always subject to blame.

When she got to her office, Claire checked her voice mail and heard Avery Dunstan ask her to call him ASAP. With Avery everything was ASAP, so she set the message aside and made a list of people she had to call, trying to limit it to those who absolutely needed to know about Tim's death, eliminating those she merely wanted to commiserate with. Ada Vail should be told. Jennie Dell had an interest and should also be notified. Tim's mother, Vivian Sansevera, already knew, of course, but Claire wanted to express her sympathy. She thought about calling Vivian, but decided to write a note instead. Harrison, who was last on her list, was the person who would need to be notified first. Claire walked down the hallway to his office.

He had just arrived and was hanging his hat and scarf on a rack as she knocked on the door. When he turned around to answer her summons, she noticed he hadn't put his library face on yet. He looked disheveled and windblown. His features didn't have their usual locked-jaw severity, reminding Claire that he had a life outside of the center—a wife, whom she had never met, and children—although he always gave the impression that he lived alone. He had trouble finding his voice, as if this were the first time he had spoken this morning.

"Claire," he said, clearing his throat. "How was Utah?" Someone else might have smiled at this point, but Harrison's face settled into its typically remote expression.

"I have bad news," Claire said.

"Oh?" Harrison scowled, remembering perhaps the last time Claire had returned to the center with bad news.

"Tim Sansevera died in Sin Nombre Canyon."

"Good grief! How did that happen?"

"It appears he fell from a ledge."

"Was he alone?"

"Apparently. He spent the night in the canyon. When he didn't show up to meet Curt and me, we hiked in and found the body near his campsite."

"Were you able to recover any of Jonathan Vail's effects?"

"No. We had directions to the cave, but when we got there,

it was empty."

"How disappointing," Harrison said.

Considering that a promising graduate student had lost his life, "disappointing" struck Claire as the wrong choice of words.

"So now all we have to verify Tim's story is the journal?"

"True."

"It's still possible the journal is a hoax."

"Ada Vail believed the writing was authentic," Claire reminded him, "and so did I."

"I'll give Ada a call about this."

Claire made a mental note to cross that name off her list.

"I think it's past time to have the manuscript authenticated. I'll call August Stevenson." He was a handwriting expert who had retired to Santa Fe.

"All right."

Harrison sat down at his desk. He collected folk art, and there was a papier-mâché skeleton of death pulling a cart on the shelf behind his head. Claire had the sensation that death was grinning at her over Harrison's shoulder. He waved a long white hand and dismissed her.

Claire turned to leave, noticing that the windows up near the ceiling of Harrison's office were deep blue rectangles, as if the walls were framing the sky in a series of abstractions. In Utah she felt she could reach out and touch the sky. In Harrison's office it seemed impossibly remote.

When she got back to her own office, she crossed Ada Vail off her list. She was looking for Jennie Dell's number when she sensed someone at her window and looked up to see Avery Dunstan standing there, although even when standing still he appeared to be in motion. He waved at Claire, then opened her door and let himself in.

"Sorry I didn't get back to you sooner," Claire said. "I just returned from Utah and I had to talk to Harrison."

Avery was so intent on what he had to say that her comments made no impression. He stood in front of her desk, cocked his head, and looked down at his nose.

"I had to come over here to look something up. I wanted to tell you about a strange meeting I had with Tim Sansevera."

"When?"

"Late Thursday, just before I went home."

"Avery, there's something I . . ."

Claire hesitated just long enough for Avery to catch his breath and rush on. "He was very insistent that we publish the journal word for word, and furious at Ada Vail for intervening. He wants his name on the book. Why is he so intense about this? Since we don't even have a contract to publish the journal, it strikes me as premature to be discussing how we are going to edit it and whose name goes where."

It seemed insignificant to Claire as she explained to Avery what had happened.

"That's awful!" Avery shivered. "How old was he?"

"Thirty."

"Obviously the journal was something he cared about very much, far beyond the usual graduate student obsession. You don't suppose there is any possibility that . . ."

Claire, who was expecting Avery to suggest forgery, was startled when he said, "Tim is Jonathan Vail's son."

Actually the idea *had* occurred to Claire. She saw a resemblance between them in appearance and in temperament, but she had dismissed the father/son connection as too far-fetched. "I have no reason to believe that," she said.

"He's the right age, isn't he?"

"Yes."

"Anglo looks, Spanish surname. Could be his mother was Indian or Hispanic. He took the mother's name, but his father was Vail. You've heard all the rumors, I'm sure."

"I've heard a lot of them. I don't know that I've heard *all* of them," Claire said.

"It would explain the obsession," Avery replied. "Wouldn't it? Maybe he didn't find the journal in the cave. Maybe he found it in a family closet or garage."

"Then why invent a story about finding it in Sin Nombre Canyon?"

"Far more romantic than finding it in a garage, isn't it?"

"Why lure us up there?"

"Once he told the lie, he'd have to follow through, wouldn't he?" Avery said.

Claire knew that in his spare time he was writing a novel. With his imagination, perhaps he should be writing fiction instead of editing fact.

"Are you sure the death was accidental?" he asked.

"No, but the rangers are investigating."

Avery picked up the glass paperweight that lay on Claire's desk and tossed it from one hand to the other. "It could change things in terms of publishing the journal," he said. "If Tim was Jonathan's son and someone else was Tim's heir, maybe we wouldn't have to deal with Ada Vail."

"That's a very remote possibility," Claire said, feeling a duty to pull Avery back to earth.

"Worth checking out, though, isn't it?"

"I have the address of Tim's mother," Claire said. "I plan to get in touch with her."

"Good!" said Avery.

"How did Tim seem when you talked to him? Was he anxious or fearful?"

"He seemed determined," Avery said. "Gotta run."

He put the paperweight back on the desk and rushed out of the room.

Claire composed a handwritten letter to Vivian Sansevera, explaining who she was and expressing her deepest sympathy. She closed by asking Vivian to give her a call.

She dialed Jennie Dell's number and wasn't terribly surprised to learn that Curt Devereux had already told her about Tim's death. "Ironic, isn't it," Jennie said, "that a person so devoted to Jonathan's work should lose his life in the same place Jonathan lost his?"

"Did Curt tell you how Tim died?" Claire asked.

"He said that he fell from a ledge. That canyon is a very treacherous place to climb, and not a good place to be alone. Once I realized Jonathan wasn't coming back, I got out of there as soon as I could."

"How did you get out?"

"I hiked over the mesa. The canyon was flooded. When I got to the road, I hitched a ride to the ranger station. That's when I met Curt."

"It's hard to find your way across the mesa, isn't it?" Claire asked.

"It was easier back then. The Hopi still went into the canyon to leave offerings, and I followed one of their trails."

"I stopped to see Sam Ogelthorpe on my way home."

"Is that old coot still alive?" Jennie asked.

"Still alive and still insisting that he saw Jonathan killing one of his cows two days before you reported him missing."

"He was half blind then. He's probably totally blind now. If he saw anything it was a mountain lion. He keeps telling this story because he loves the attention. Trust me, Jonathan Vail did not get out of Sin Nombre Canyon. Jonathan died there."

"Curt and I went to the cave where Tim said he found the journal, but we didn't find the duffel bag Tim had mentioned."

"As I said, there wasn't any duffel bag."

"Since Tim wasn't there to show us, I wasn't sure we went to the right cave, although Jonathan's initials were carved in the wall."

"Jonathan's initials were carved in walls all over the canyons, occasionally by him, more often by other people. I know that he was more likely to go into caves that didn't look like they'd been used by Indians. He considered the Indian caves sacred ground. Listen, Claire," she said, changing the subject, "Lou Bastiann is coming for Veterans Day this year. He's very devoted to Jonathan's work, and I'm going to show him the journal and see what he thinks about publication."

It wasn't what Ada would want, but since Curt had given Jennie a copy of the journal, Claire didn't see how she could prevent it.

"I'll call you after he's seen it," Jennie said.

"All right," Claire replied and hung up. Now that she had done her job and worked her way through her list, she felt she could allow herself some respite, and she decided to stop by and see John Harlan after work. He was an old friend and an antiquarian bookseller. His wife had died the year before Claire got divorced. They had dinner together occasionally, and though sometimes Claire sensed that John would like to go beyond friendship, he hadn't made any definite moves in that direction. When her husband left her for a graduate student named Melissa, she built a shell around her heart. She didn't expect to have it forever, but she didn't know how to get rid of it either. A shell could dissolve, flake off, or shatter. Crisis was one way to crack it open, and she had just been through one. She knew John cared enough to listen with sympathy, and he also had a good bullshit detector. There were many elements about the disappearance of Jonathan Vail and the death of Tim Sansevera that took those events out of the black-and-white realm of reality and into the shadowy world of fiction. Maybe John could make them real again.

On her way home, she stopped at Page One, Too, the bookstore where John worked. She found him with his feet up on his desk, his computer turned off, surrounded by price guides and books. John hated the computer and he kept a messy office. His shirt was wrinkled and his hair needed cutting, but she found his rumpled appearance comforting. He dropped his feet to the floor and stood up when he saw her. John was six feet tall, but lean as a greyhound. In fact, when Claire hugged him she felt his bones.

"I hear you just made the find of the century," he said. "The journal of Jonathan Vail, intact after all this time!"

It had been over a week. Claire should have known that everybody in the business would know about the journal by now. Did John know about Tim's death, too? She wondered. If so, he gave no sign.

"I didn't make the find. A graduate student did."

"Yeah, but he brought it to you, right? You're the archivist. Hell, you're the one who's going to get the credit. Have you had the manuscript authenticated yet?"

"Harrison called August Stevenson."

"He's the best," John said. "This is going to give your career a major boost, so why the long face?"

Tim's death was one piece of news that hadn't made its way to John's office yet. "That's awful," he said when Claire told him. "Let's go out to dinner. It'll take your mind off it for a little while."

She agreed, and they drove down the street in their separate vehicles to Emilio's, where John ordered a huge bowl of spaghetti and Claire got a salad. It was all she could stomach at the moment. John ate his spaghetti by wrapping it in his fork and twirling it on his spoon, splattering sauce all over the tablecloth. When he was finished, he put down the fork and the spoon and asked, "It's the twilight zone, isn't it? The grad student dying in the same place his hero died."

"I don't know that Jonathan died there, do you?"

"It's what I've always suspected. He's a legend. If he were alive, he'd let the world know about it."

"I suppose," Claire said. "I stopped to talk to Sam Ogelthorpe, and he raised the possibility that Jonathan might have died somewhere else. Mexico, for example."

"I envy you, going all these places, meeting all these mythical characters. How about Jennie Dell? Have you met her yet?"

"Yes."

"If Jonathan died in Slickrock Canyon, you've gotta believe she played a role. Does she live up to her reputation?"

Claire had a pretty good idea of what he was talking about, but she asked anyway. "And what reputation is that?"

"That she's a woman who might be worth dyin' for."

"Not in my opinion," Claire said. "Maybe she's gotten tamer as she's gotten older. She calls herself a house cat now."

"Happens to the best of us." John sighed.

"Did you know that she published a novel?"

"No. When?"

"She didn't say."

"I'd like to read it."

"I'm sure you would," Claire replied. The check arrived and she reached for it, but John grabbed it first.

"It's on me," he said.

He walked her to her car and gave her a hug before they parted. He'd been sympathetic. He'd helped put recent events in perspective. She just wished they hadn't ended up talking about Jennie Dell.

8

Chapter Eight

Ordinarily it took weeks to get August Stevenson to authenticate a document, but for Jonathan Vail's notebook he drove down to the center immediately. Claire always enjoyed seeing August, who seemed very comfortable in his seventy-five-year-old skin. Ten years earlier he'd moved to Santa Fe from New York City after a distinguished career in document verification. He had accomplished everything an expert could accomplish in his field. He established that a series of letters from Marilyn Monroe to John Kennedy was a fake, proved that there were far more copies of the Texas State Constitution in circulation than there were in existence, and perfected a method of pollen dating for documents. Previously pollen had been used only to date archaeological finds, but August proved that it could be used to date manuscripts as well. He claimed to be retired, but that only meant that documents found their way to him in Santa Fe rather than in New York. Claire considered the center fortunate to have him living only sixty miles away.

She'd gone for a cup of coffee and was returning to her office when she saw August making his way down the hall. He had a broad back and a lumbering walk that made her think of a turtle. August didn't carry his home on his back, he carried the weight of his knowledge, but that was all he needed to operate anywhere in the world. He wore dark lenses over his regular glasses to shield his eyes from the New Mexico sun. When he came inside, he flipped the dark lenses up so they stuck straight out, framing and emphasizing his eyes like an actress's theatrical eyelashes or a turtle's hooded lids.

"Hello, August," Claire called to him. She knew he admired her work, and he always treated her with the utmost respect, yet his ponderous way of moving made her feel like a schoolgirl, like she might start skipping down the hallway if she didn't contain herself. Although August was preeminent in his field, his only degree was a B.A. in English Literature from Columbia, so he didn't have the self-important manner of some of the scholars Claire worked with.

"Good afternoon, Claire," he said in a gravely voice. He had given up smoking when he retired and developed a hoarseness in his throat that had never gone away. Claire stepped aside and let him negotiate his way into her office and lower himself into a chair. He carried a leather briefcase with brass fittings, and he placed it on the floor next to the chair. The thickness of the lenses in his clear glasses made his eyes appear enormous, over-sized eyes framed by oversized lashes with an expression that could be read from the very back row.

"What a remarkable find!" he began. "If the journal *is* Jonathan Vail's. I can't think of a document that has been more sought after in the Southwest in my lifetime."

"A graduate student named Tim Sansevera found it and brought it to me."

"Ah, yes, and now he is dead, Harrison told me, and in the very same place where Vail disappeared. Not a good omen for the document or the messenger, would you say?"

Claire chose her words carefully. She imagined that someone who assigned so much weight to the way words looked would also be acutely aware of their meaning. "Tim's death could be accidental. The rangers are investigating."

"Rangers may see death often, but murder rarely. They should call in the FBI."

"They intend to, if they find anything suspicious."

"And if I find something suspicious? A man who dies after delivering a forged document is more likely to be the victim of foul play than a man who dies after delivering an authentic document, wouldn't you say?"

Claire felt he was testing her. He had made the equivalent of a chess move that, if she was careless, would call out her ego or her queen. "Not necessarily. In this case, an authentic document could reveal what actually happened to Jonathan Vail, but a forgery would have to be considered fiction."

"If the manuscript turns out to be authentic, I will leave the contents to you to make sense of. Let's take a look at it."

"I'll bring it to you in the Anderson Reading Room."

August maneuvered his bulk to the edge of the chair. Claire watched while he gathered the strength to push himself up, wondering if she should offer to help. He rocked back, forward, then back again, gaining momentum. He pushed hard and was on his feet, leading with the dark lenses and toting his briefcase in his hand.

Claire led him to the Anderson Reading Room, where Gail

Benton sat at the reference desk, dressed in another forgettable little dress. Gail's wardrobe ranged from shades of pale gray to shades of deep brown, the colors of an inconspicuous little bird. She took her Ph.D. seriously, but her job at the moment was to check ID's before granting access to valuable papers. She did it with a deliberateness that demonstrated she considered the work beneath her. Claire thought Gail might forgo the formality once August Stevenson was introduced, but the introduction only made her actions more annoyingly deliberate. She certainly should know who August was, but she didn't let on, treating him like an overaged grad student and demanding that he surrender his ID, which she intended to hold as long as he was in the Anderson Reading Room. August grudgingly complied.

"You must also leave your briefcase at the desk," Gail said.

"I have been hired to authenticate a document," August replied in his raspy voice, which he dropped a couple of decibels so Gail had to lean closer to hear. "My briefcase contains the tools of my trade. Without it, I am rendered ineffective and unable to work."

Gail looked to Claire for confirmation. "Harrison has given him permission to examine the Jonathan Vail notebook," Claire said.

Gail hesitated, willing enough to challenge Claire's authority but not so willing to take on Harrison. "What are your tools?" she asked August.

"A camera, calipers, rulers, a pollen-collecting kit."

"You may take them inside," Gail said. "But the briefcase remains here, and you must wear our white gloves."

August glared at Gail from beneath the dark, protruding lenses. "I brought my own gloves. Perfectly white and never washed in detergent."

August took his tools from his briefcase, while Claire went

to get the notebook. When she returned he was sitting at a table wearing his white gloves. She brought the notebook to him inside the thick gray briefcase, which lost a little more dust in transition. She also brought the manuscript of *A Blue-Eyed Boy*, which was typed but had Jonathan's handwritten notes in the margin, as well as the handwritten manuscript of the earlier journal, so August could compare Jonathan's writing at various stages of his life.

"Interesting hide," he said, fingering the side of the briefcase with his white-gloved fingers.

"Buffalo?" Claire asked.

"I don't think so. Buffalo is more supple."

"It may have been in a cave for many years and stiffened."

"Taking that into account, I still don't believe it's buffalo. I'll take some measurement and photographs. The zipper and the style of the briefcase may give me some indication of where it came from. I'll try to capture some pollen and do some comparisons when I get home." With his white-gloved fingers, he slid the notebook out of the briefcase. "This type of spiralbound notebook was used by college students in the sixties," he said. "The color of the paper, the dryness, the brittle quality indicate age and a dry climate, but paper can be artificially aged. Was the cave where this was found sealed? A sealed cave would help to preserve the paper."

"There were indications that a rock slide closed the cave and that another slide opened it again."

"The ink is all from a ball-point pen, possibly a Bic. They were in use in the sixties. If the handwriting appears to be Vail's, we'll discuss the possibility of dating the paper and the ink. Exactly when this was written could be important to both the center and the investigation."

Very important, Claire thought, but she doubted Harrison

or Ada Vail would allow the notebook to leave the library. "Something I found puzzling is that there are places where the handwriting gets larger and sloppier," she told August.

"I'll look into it. And now, if you don't mind, I'd like to spend some time with Madam Librarian . . ." He peered through his thick lenses at Gail. "And Mr. Vail."

"Take all the time you want. I'll be waiting in my office," Claire said.

She left August hovering over the manuscript like a jeweler inspecting a precious gem and returned to her desk. She tried to work, but found it difficult to concentrate. In her mind her reputation was on the line, since she had stated she believed the journal to be authentic. Tim's posthumous reputation was also on the line. If the manuscript was a forgery, it was highly unlikely that he came across it by accident in a cave. Harrison was always noncommittal enough to protect his own reputation. If the journal were proven to be a forgery, the center would have a document that was valuable only as a curiosity, Tim's death would be even more suspicious, and the dark hole surrounding the disappearance of Jonathan Vail would grow deeper. If the journal were proven to be a forgery, it would also become a work of fiction; any clues it contained would have to be considered worthless, even if the forger turned out to be someone familiar with Vail.

Claire spent most of the afternoon doodling on a notepad. She was prepared to stay until the Anderson Reading Room closed, but August surprised her by showing up at five, lowering himself into her chair, and placing his briefcase on the floor beside him. Had it been anyone else, Claire might have suspected him of smuggling the journal out in his briefcase in spite of the vigilance of Gail, the library's guard dog. A thief might even have considered circumnavigating her a challenge.

So might August, but Claire knew he wouldn't act on it. Reputation was everything in his field.

He seemed tired to Claire as he sank into the chair, but his eyes shimmered with intelligence behind the thick lenses. "At last I was able to wrest my briefcase and ID from the grip of Madam Librarian," he said. "I can once again prove that I am August Stevenson."

"I didn't doubt it for minute," Claire responded. "What did you find?"

August seemed to withdraw into his shell, turning as cautious as a lawyer. "I'd like to test the ink and the paper, if you can persuade Harrison to let me take the journal from the library."

"It will be difficult," Claire replied. "The manuscript is here at the discretion of Jonathan's mother, who doesn't want it to leave the center. I could give you a photocopy to take with you if you want to study the handwriting further."

"I'd like that," August said. "Based on a preliminary examination of the handwriting, comparing it to the earlier writing, I will say that I do believe the journal to be the work of Jonathan Vail. The way the letters float above the line is a sign of vanity. The loops of the L's, the carelessness of the capital C, the curlicues in the W's, the sloppy punctuation—all are indications of Jonathan's unreliable temperament."

"Thank God," said Claire.

"It means a lot to you, doesn't it?"

"A lot. What did you think about the places where the writing got larger? Could that have been the work of someone else?"

"I don't believe so. It's Jonathan's script, albeit in an exaggerated form. In my opinion it is the writing of Vail under the influence of a drug, quite possibly a hallucinatory drug, considering the time in which it was written. I may never be able to date it exactly but I believe the journal was written in the sixties by Vail and only by Vail. Personally, I always considered him a fiction writer even when he wasn't under the influence of drugs. It's easy to be self-serving and sensitive in a memoir and a coming-of-age novel. He had a rebelliousness that matched the times, but what did he actually do, other than mouth off and disappear? Whether you and the investigators take the content of this notebook as truth or as fiction is up to you. I would believe him when he says he had rice and beans for dinner and that he disliked his mother, but as for the rest of it . . ."

"May I submit your preliminary finding to the investigators?"

"You may. I will prepare a full report for the center."

"And the briefcase?"

"That will require further investigation. I have taken photographs and measurements. I was able to find a few microscopic grains of pollen in the seam, which I will try to locate and date. I presume that no one minds if some pollen leaves the library?"

It was a rhetorical question, and he didn't wait for an answer. "I will be in touch when I have completed my investigation. Should I submit my preliminary findings to Harrison before I leave?"

"Of course," said Claire.

August pushed himself out of his chair and picked up his briefcase. She led him down the hallway and discovered, with a certain amount of pleasure, that Harrison had left for the day. She bade good-bye to August, retrieved the notebook from the Anderson Reading Room, and locked it in the safe for the night.

When she got home she went to her courtyard, sat down on the banco, and thought about what August had said while she waited for her datura to bloom. It was the end of the season, and the only reason this datura was still blooming was that it had a sunny, sheltered spot. Datura was a member of the deadly nightshade family, and its seeds were hallucinogenic and poisonous if not prepared properly.

Claire knew that it grew all over the Southwest and as far east as North Carolina. Most likely it grew in Utah, too. Even if it didn't, Jennie or Jonathan could have brought the seeds or another hallucinogen into the canyon. A hallucinogen would explain the exaggerated handwriting and the description of the canyon walls slipping and sliding like La Sagrada Familia. It could also explain what had happened to Jonathan: he might have been poisoned or fallen while under the influence, and Jennie was too involved to want to admit it. Tim might have taken drugs, too, but at least that would show up in the autopsy.

August had pretty much established that the journal was authentic, even if he hadn't completed his report. Claire knew that what he initially saw in a document tended to be supported by further analysis. The fact that the journal was authentic would support Tim's story and increase the likelihood that there really had been a duffel bag. Where had it gone? Claire wondered. What was in it? Was Jennie lying when she said she hadn't seen a duffel bag, or had Jonathan brought it into the cave without her knowledge? Claire wished she had some way of establishing Jennie's veracity. Not trusting her added confusion to this investigation.

Datura was a night bloomer. The flowers opened when the sun went down. It was an event as predictable and magical as the full moon rising at sunset, but it always filled Claire with awe. New Mexico was known for its brilliant sunlight and spectacular sunsets, but she loved the velvety nights here almost as much as the days.

The shadows in the courtyard deepened. The datura prepared to bloom. It turned trumpet shaped when it opened, about six inches long. At the moment the petals folded around each other and were the color of parchment, tinted lavender at the end, but when the flower opened it would be white satin. Now the shape was protruding and male. Once it bloomed it would turn receptive and female. In the morning, the spent flower faded, drooped, and became male all over again. The role reversal was part of the plant's mystery. Even without hallucinogenic properties, it was magical. Georgia O'Keeffe celebrated datura in her paintings—and rightly so, Claire thought.

She had always been aware of datura in the desert, but this was the first time she'd had the opportunity to study one up close in all its phases. Her plant could be a volunteer, a seed that had blown into her courtyard from somewhere else, a gift of the wind. With no attention from her, the vines had extended four feet into the courtyard and three feet up the wall. She knew she should cut it back, but she couldn't bring herself to do it; the flowers were too beautiful. When she thought of all the plants she had fertilized, watered, sprayed, and coaxed to bloom, this one was a wild and beautiful gift. If she was ever going to have another relationship with a man, she'd want to see how he'd react to her datura. She wondered if John would appreciate the beauty. Her ex-husband, Evan, had considered it a noxious weed, and when one tried to establish itself in their yard in Tucson, he yanked it out.

In the summer the plant was full of flowers, but tonight there were only two buds, possibly the last flowers of the season. Claire couldn't see the sun from where she sat, but she could feel it drop behind the west mesa. The temperature fell, as it always did at nightfall in the desert. The antennae at the end of the buds began to quiver. A moth came out of the shadows and hovered, waiting for the blossoms to open. Bees buzzed and competed for space. To actually see a flower bloom seemed so miraculous to Claire that she never quite believed it would happen. She was astonished, as always, when the flowers burst open, white as wedding dresses, releasing a lush, delicate fragrance that drove the bees to distraction.

9

Chapter Nine

Jennie had told Claire she would call when Lou Bastiann had read the journal, but the call actually came from Lou himself. Claire had known nothing about him before she read the journal, and all she knew now was that he was a fan and a vet. He had never assumed the legendary status of the other figures in the Vail history.

He cleared his throat as he introduced himself. "I've read the journal," he said. "I'd like to get together with you to talk about it."

"All right," Claire agreed.

"There's a bar I've been to called Tom's, near the university. Do you know it?"

Claire had never been to Tom's, but she knew where it was, and she agreed to meet him there after work. When she arrived, there were a couple of cars in the parking lot and a motorcycle with Missouri plates. Inside, it took a minute for her eyes to make the adjustment from the late-afternoon sun to the darkness. During that time she stood in the doorway feeling exposed, visible to whoever was in the bar before anyone else was visible to her.

A voice came out of the shadows. "Claire?" the man asked.

"Lou?"

"That's me." He grinned, and Claire saw that he was missing a tooth. By now her eyes had adjusted well enough to take a good look at Lou Bastiann. He was her height. A few years older—or he might have lived a harder life. He had a middle-aged spread, a pasty complexion, and a gray beard, yet his arms were muscular and strong as if he was a laborer or worked out with weights. He wore a black T-shirt, black jeans, and motorcycle boots. It was a uniform of sorts, but Lou's looks were average enough that they would have adapted almost as well to a business suit. Tom's had a sawdust floor and a long bar that, at the moment, was empty. The mirror behind it reflected no one's face. Lou led Claire past the bar to the table in the back where he'd been sitting. He held his left leg stiff as he walked, which made her wonder if he had been wounded in Vietnam.

There were a couple of empty Miller Lite bottles on the table. "Care for a beer?" he asked.

"I'd prefer a white wine."

He went to the bar to get it.

"I envy you," he said when he returned. "Keeping the archives for Jonathan Vail. What an interesting job!"

"It hasn't been so wonderful lately."

"Yeah. Jennie told me about the grad student. That's a tough one."

Lou Bastiann had restless eyes that lit briefly on Claire before roaming around the room. A ray of sunshine had come in through a window and was spotlighting the dusty floor. Lou's eyes went to the light but didn't linger. They were dark brown, almost black, the color of a butterfly that Claire saw occasionally in her courtyard.

"It's always good to be back in New Mexico," he said. "The light here. It's like nowhere else in the world."

Claire sipped at her drink, a house wine, most likely cheap Chardonnay. It would take a couple of glasses before it started tasting good. "Do you come to New Mexico often?"

"Whenever I can. I like to go to the Vietnam Memorial in Angel Fire for Veterans Day. Have you ever been?"

"Yes, but not on Veterans Day."

"It's a powerful ceremony, a way of remembering the guys who didn't make it back."

"You were in Vietnam when Jonathan disappeared?" Claire asked, while trying, unsuccessfully, to place him in one of the two categories of Vietnam vets she knew: the ones who were destroyed by the experience and the ones who showed no ill effects. Lou had an unfinished quality. He wasn't a street person, but he didn't look as if he'd settled into a comfortable middle age, either. Her impression was the jury was still out on his life.

"Yes," he said. "Jonathan was my hero. I was in boot camp when *A Blue-Eyed Boy* came out. It took a while for that book to become popular, but I read it immediately. I was full of doubts about the war, but when I got drafted I went. That's what people did in Missouri, where I come from. Jonathan, he was free, living in the desert, protesting the war. That was what I wanted to be doing, and I also wanted to be a writer. It made me feel good that someone was living the life I wanted, instead of going off to Vietnam to dodge bullets. I wrote him, and he wrote me back right away. His letters kept me going. I didn't have a girlfriend back home or a family to write to."

"Do you still have the letters?"

"Sure do," Lou said, taking a sip of his beer.

"The center would love to have them."

"I'd hate to part with them, but I'll tell you what . . ." Lou grinned. "I'll leave them to the center when I die."

"Did you become a writer?"

"No, I didn't."

"What do you do?" Claire asked.

"I'm an auto mechanic. It was hard for me to write after the war. Besides, I knew I could never write anything as good as *A Blue-Eyed Boy*. Tell me something. What do the scholars at UNM think of *A Blue-Eyed Boy*? Has it held up over time?" His eyes stopped on her face and lingered there until Claire answered the question.

"It is still considered a classic."

"I'm glad," Lou replied. "And the journal? What did you think of the writing there?"

"In all honesty, I don't think it measures up to *A Blue-Eyed Boy*. But it is a journal, not a novel. It was written in the canyons under difficult circumstances, possibly under the influence of drugs."

"Jennie said it was found in a briefcase?"

"It was."

"Could you tell me what it looked like?"

"It was pretty dusty after being in the cave all this time. It was made out of a thick gray hide I couldn't identify. It had a zipper. There was a pouch inside."

Lou put his beer bottle down on the table with a thump. "Damn! That pleases me. I sent Jonathan that briefcase from Vietnam. It's made out of elephant hide, and I bought it on Tu

Do Street in Saigon in 1966. I was in army intelligence then, under shallow cover, which meant I wore civilian dress and wasn't allowed to carry a weapon. I bought a .38 on the black market and kept it in that pouch. When I got shipped out to Hue, I didn't need the briefcase anymore, so I sent it to Jonathan."

"Did you also send him a duffel bag?"

"No. I don't know anything about a duffel bag. The rangers are investigating, aren't they?"

"Yes."

"How's it going?" His butterfly eyes had begun to wander again. Claire wondered if they would be so restless if he hadn't had several beers.

"They haven't found anything new as far as I know."

"Do you think it will hurt Jonathan's reputation to publish the journal as it is?"

"That's not my decision to make."

"But if it were?"

"I think it's a historical document that should be published word for word. If I could, I'd keep the dust, the careless handwriting, the grammatical errors, everything. I believe Jonathan's fans and scholars will accept the imperfections. But Ada Vail owns the rights, and whoever publishes it has to honor her wishes."

"Ada Vail's heart is made out of concrete. What does her husband think?"

"There's no way of telling. He's had a stroke, and he doesn't speak anymore."

"I think if Jonathan were here, his choice would be to publish it as is, don't you? It's an expression of what he saw and felt at the time. He'd want you to do everything you could to keep the journal intact."

"There isn't much I can do."

"You're his archivist, aren't you? The person responsible for preserving his legend?"

"Yes, but I'm not his publisher, and I don't own the rights to his work."

"Sometimes people can do more than they think they can," Lou said.

"I'll try," Claire told him, "But I can't make any promises."

"Well, it has been great to meet you." Lou stood up and gave her a firm handshake with a palm that felt rough and callused. "Thanks a lot for your time."

"You're welcome to come to the center and look at the Vail papers whenever you like."

"I may just take you up on that," Lou said.

They walked out to the parking lot together. Lou put on his helmet, got on his motorcycle, and drove away while Claire was still inserting her key in her ignition. By the time he reached Central, she was wishing she'd asked how she could reach him.

The next morning she called August Stevenson and reported what Lou had told her about the briefcase.

"That's consistent with what I've discovered so far," he replied. "I consulted a leather expert and determined that the hide is elephant. Considering when the journal was written, the likely source would be southeast Asia, in particular, Vietnam. Elephants are endangered now, and the hide can no longer be legally sold, but that wasn't the case in the sixties. Briefcases like this one were common. GI's bought them on Tu Do Street as souvenirs. I haven't had a chance to do it yet, but a pollen analysis would date it and establish for certain where it came from."

"I don't think it will be necessary," Claire said, mindful of how tight Harrison was with the center's money. "I think you have enough information to submit your report now."

"I'll get it in the mail this afternoon," August replied.

Claire thanked him and hung up. Knowing Harrison would be out of the library all day at a conference, she went to his office, opened the safe, put on a pair of white gloves, and took out the briefcase. It made sense that the weathered gray hide was elephant. She wondered why she hadn't thought of that herself. She unzipped the zipper and slid her hand inside the pouch that Lou had described. She had once held a Ladysmith .38 that her friend Madeline kept for protection; it would have fit comfortably in this pouch. Saigon had been an elegant city. She could imagine a younger, smoother Lou Bastiann strolling the streets, clutching the elephant-hide briefcase with his weapon inside.

Chapter Ten

Harrison received August's report and set up a meeting with Claire and Ada Vail in the food court to discuss it. Claire arrived at twelve-fifteen, the appointed time, but when she got to the cafeteria, Harrison and Ada were already sitting at a table in the window eating. She felt a flash of annoyance. Had he done this to embarrass her or because he wanted to talk about her to Ada before she arrived? Ada was jabbing her fork at Harrison to make a point when Claire walked up to the table. He noticed her approach and stood up. A courtesy Claire could not remember having received before. She attributed this display of good manners to the presence of Ada Vail. Harrison's and Ada's plates were full, but Claire had lost her appetite.

"Good of you to join us," Harrison said.

Ada remained seated, but extended her hand. Claire took it, said hello, and sat down at the table.

"Do you plan to get something to eat?" Harrison asked.

"I'm not hungry," Claire replied.

Ada wore a black dress and a red-and-black scarf knotted around her neck. Her hair was pulled straight back. There were bright dots of rouge on each cheek, the sign of an older woman whose eyesight is failing.

"Don't let me interrupt you," Claire said, knowing full well that her own courtesy to Ada was being graded by Harrison. One would think that well-educated people would learn good manners somewhere along the way, but Claire knew the opposite was often the case. The more advanced the degree, the ruder the person was likely to be. Rudeness from someone who should know better came with a capital *R*.

Ada had sliced her chicken breast into tiny pieces. She speared one with her fork and held it in suspension between her plate and her mouth. "Harrison said your handwriting expert confirmed that the notebook is Jonathan's."

"Based on a handwriting analysis, he believes it's Jonathan's," Claire said. It was a slight correction, but would Harrison consider it a discourtesy? She resisted the temptation to look for his reaction and kept her eyes focused on Ada. "August could do some tests on the paper to date it, but that would mean taking the notebook out of the library."

Ada put her chicken down on her plate. "Is that necessary?" she asked.

"Not at all," Harrison said, soothing her.

"Anything could happen to the notebook if it leaves the center."

"August has impeccable credentials," Claire replied. "I have full confidence in him."

"We all believe the manuscript to be authentic," Ada insisted.

"True," Claire said. "August has established that the briefcase came from Vietnam and is made out of elephant hide. I met with Lou Bastiann."

"He's the Lou who is mentioned in the journal?"

"Yes."

"Was he one of Jonathan's antiwar friends?" The piece of chicken had made its way to Ada's mouth, and she began chewing on it.

"No. He's a fan of Jonathan's who served in Vietnam. He told me he sent the briefcase to Jonathan from Saigon. When he came back he looked Jennie up. They've stayed in touch over the years."

"Many of Jonathan's fans looked *me* up after he disappeared," Ada said.

"Of course they would. You're his mother," Harrison said in a soothing-as-Pabulum voice. Claire was glad she hadn't gotten any food. Anything chewed on at this table would taste like mush. "Ada is concerned about the death of Tim Sansevera," he told Claire.

"We all are," Claire said. "I wrote to his mother and expressed the center's deepest sympathy. I'm hoping we can get together when she feels up to it."

"Curt Devereux got to Slickrock Canyon before you?" Ada asked, fixing her sharp black eyes on Claire.

"Yes."

"Do you know when?"

"Not exactly."

"He should have gone back for that duffel bag the minute he heard it was there. Has it occurred to you that he may have had something to do with the young man's death? Curt bungled the investigation of Jonathan's disappearance. Perhaps the duffel bag contained a clue that would prove his incompetence and connect him to Jennie Dell."

It was a thought that continued to occur to Claire, coming out of the night like a moth and disappearing back into it again. "Ellen Frank, the ranger who is investigating Tim's death, seems to know what she is doing," she said.

"I wouldn't trust the rangers to investigate one of their own," Ada declared. When she got angry, the red spots on her cheeks turned redder, making the rest of her skin appear powdery white. "I've asked Nick Lorenz, my private investigator, to look into it. He'll get in touch with you."

Claire was intrigued by the prospect of meeting Nick, another character who seemed to be popping out of the pages of the Jonathan Vail history book. "In all the reported sightings of Jonathan, did Nick ever find any proof that he was still alive?"

"No," Ada said. "Which is why I came to believe my son died in Slickrock Canyon, that Jennie Dell was responsible, and that Curt Devereux is protecting her."

"Did Nick find any evidence that Jonathan left an heir?"

"No," Ada said again.

Claire intended to ask Nick Lorenz the very same questions, wondering if his answers would be so unequivocal. With any luck, Harrison wouldn't be present and she wouldn't be constrained by his notions of politeness. Coaxing money and cooperation from a benefactor resembled walking on eggs. She could do it when she had to, but she'd rather be doing something else. She hoped to meet Nick as far away from Ada, Harrison, and the university as possible.

"Ada and I have been discussing publication of the journal," Harrison said, tearing at a piece of bread with his long fingers. His eyes turned into warning lights across the table, and Claire understood why he had arranged for her to arrive late. "Now that it has been authenticated, Ada has agreed to allow UNM Press to publish it. The university, of course, is extremely pleased. Ada will act as an adviser."

Adviser, Claire wondered, or hatchet woman? "Will Avery be the editor?" she asked.

"The committee hasn't decided yet." Harrison's position as head of the center automatically gave him a spot on the UNM Press Review Committee and the power to approve or veto any project. Claire doubted that Avery would want the job under Ada Vail's conditions. "Since you are a Vail expert, we would like you to contribute in some way," Harrison said to Claire. "To write an introduction, perhaps."

"Perhaps," said Claire. "If you will excuse me, I'm going to get something to eat." If there was anything she didn't want to do at the moment, it was eat, but a trip through the cafeteria line would take her away from the table.

"Certainly," said Harrison.

Claire walked to the other end of the cafeteria and made her way through the food line, dawdling in front of the salads, weighing the worth of vinegar and oil versus Thousand Island, hesitating before the main course (chicken breast? beefsteak?), considering and reconsidering what she would drink. By the time she returned to the table, Ada and Harrison had finished their lunch and were preparing to leave. She said good-bye, sat down at the table, stared out the window, and picked at her salad.

She was tempted to call Avery when she got back to her office, but she didn't feel she'd been authorized to pass on what she'd heard. She knew it was only a matter of time before he would call her. Later that afternoon, Nick Lorenz phoned to set up an appointment.

"Where is your office?" she asked him.

"I'm semi-retired," he said. "I live in Rio Rancho. I don't go into the office as much now, but I still keep one across the river in the North Valley."

"I'll meet you there," Claire said.

"All right," Nick replied in a brusque voice that left Claire wondering whether he wanted to meet with her at all. They set up a time for later in the week.

The following morning Avery called. "Could you meet me beside the duck pond?" he asked in a whispery, conspiratorial voice. "Say in fifteen minutes?"

"I'll be there," Claire said.

She left the center, walked around the corner of the library, and sat down on a bench that faced the pond. It was one of those crisp fall days that felt more like the beginning of a season than the end of one to Claire. The leaves on the trees around the pond had changed color. A breeze brushed the surface of the water and turned the reflection to liquid gold. Her sense of having an assignation with Avery was diminished by the fact that they were meeting in plain sight—not only in plain sight but under the brilliant New Mexico sun. There were shadows and lies in New Mexico, but secrets seemed to prefer a murkier climate.

Claire watched as Avery came up the sidewalk, taking giant steps. He wore black jeans that made his legs seem even longer. His blue windbreaker flapped while he walked, as if it were an outer manifestation of an inner agitation.

"Claire," he said, taking her hand and pecking her cheek without actually looking at her. "Have you heard what the committee is planning to do with the journal? They're going to let Ada Vail decimate it."

"Harrison implied that would happen, but I didn't feel I could tell you until it became a fact."

"It's a fact," Avery said. "The committee announced their plans this morning."

"In all fairness to them, Avery, if they didn't follow Ada's wishes, she'd take the manuscript elsewhere."

"Let her," he said. "This could be the most important publication you or I will ever have a chance to be involved with, but it will have no significance whatsoever after Ada wields her scissors. A censored book is not a book the press ought to publish. They're asking me to edit it, but that's nothing more than being a production editor. Good grief!"

"Harrison mentioned my writing an introduction." It would be publishing points for Claire, but not the kind of points she wanted.

"Don't do it," Avery said.

"Do I have a choice?"

"I'd quit first," Avery said. Claire couldn't help noticing that he hadn't offered to quit *his* job. That was the control the committee had over both of them—they'd have a hard time finding jobs they liked better anywhere, much less in New Mexico. "Have you spoken to Tim Sansevera's mother yet?"

"Not yet," Claire said. "She hasn't answered my letter."

"Call her, please," Avery said taking her hand, tilting his head and looking into her eyes.

"It's a very long shot, Avery."

"It's all we have."

Claire and Avery walked to where the sidewalk divided and went their separate ways. She called Vivian Sansevera when she got back to her office and was rather relieved to get an answering machine. She left a message saying they needed to talk.

11

Chapter Eleven

Nick Lorenz's office was on Fourth Street, in a strip mall that time and development had passed by. As Albuquerque expanded, new development leapfrogged over the old. Strip malls on the edge of town replaced those closer to the center, and the new malls had a high rate of occupancy. In the older ones, parking spaces were always available, even in the middle of the day.

This mall had a mail drop, a dry cleaner, a store that sold used clothes, and a store that sold used books, but empty storefronts were spaced between them like gapped teeth. Here the storefronts were known pretentiously as "suites." For her two o'clock appointment Claire found a parking space right in front of Nick's door, a sure sign that prosperity had gone elsewhere. If she hadn't known he was semi-retired, she would have thought his business was failing. In the sixties and seventies, when he put in a lot of time for Ada Vail and presumably did do better, this sad little mall might have been on the cutting edge of the city's development. To stick with a place and a client through good times and bad could be considered a sign of character or the kind of pit-bull determination that Nick was known for.

He was keeping a low profile in his strip mall. There was no sign on the door, but he had told Claire he worked out of Suite 4. His window presented the blank face of plastic blinds closed tight. She knocked, and Nick came to the door. He was shorter than Claire, with a stocky build and a bald head circled by a ring of frizzy brown hair that reminded her of a clown's ruff. When he gripped her hand and smiled, she saw gold fillings in his teeth. He wore brown polyester pants and a short-sleeved white shirt open at the neck.

The office was done in dubious taste, with shag carpeting and fake wood paneling. Claire, who hadn't expected much in the way of decoration, was bothered more by the imitation Indian art on the walls, swirling ceremonial dancers in garish shades of orange and yellow. There was a shelf behind Nick's desk full of photographs of the private eye at various stages of his career. She wondered why Ada would hire someone with such a tacky office, but it was possible she had never been to Nick's office, that she didn't expect good taste in a private eye, or that Nick's fortunes had taken a downturn. Here was a man who had dedicated years to the search for Jonathan Vail and had come up empty. Claire had to wonder why. Was there nothing to find? Was he the wrong person to find it? Nick Lorenz might have been out of his element, an urban PI lost in the wilderness.

"Have a seat," Nick said.

Claire sat down in the chair he offered. He remained

standing behind his desk, with his hands on the back of the desk chair, as he questioned her about what she had seen in Slickrock Canyon. Her memory of that day was perfectly clear, and she relayed the events she had witnessed.

"It's possible that Curt Devereux was in the canyon with Tim Sansevera before you arrived," Nick said.

"It's possible. The rangers are investigating. I would hope they would check his alibi and establish his whereabouts."

"He has seniority, they might not. Ada doesn't have much faith in the federal government."

"I'm aware of that," Claire replied. "But right now they are the official investigators. Does anyone else have the right to intervene in an ongoing investigation?"

"Not really," Nick said. He set the chair in motion with one hand and stopped it with the other.

Claire moved to the edge of her chair, intending to change her role from inquiree to inquirer. "Did Ada give you a copy of Jonathan's journal to read?" she asked.

"Yes, and it confirmed my opinion that Jonathan and Jennie were on drugs and got careless. She was a looker. I remember the first time I saw her, at a demonstration at UNM. A band was playing and she was dancing on the stage with her long blond hair swinging. There was a woman capable of wrapping Curt Devereux around her little finger."

Nick was enjoying discussing Jennie Dell a lot more than Claire was. She changed the subject. "Did you ever go into the canyons when you were looking for Jonathan?"

"Sure. I went to Slickrock where Jennie claimed she saw him last."

"What about Sin Nombre?"

"Where is it exactly?" His hands halted the motion of the chair as he stared at Claire.

"A few miles into Slickrock toward the west."

"I think so," Nick said. "I never found any trace of Jonathan. Jennie did a good job of concealing the evidence and the body."

"By herself?" Claire asked.

"Either by herself or with the help of Curt Devereux. I never saw any evidence that anyone else was there."

But it seemed to Claire that if you accepted the premise that Jennie was capable of concealing a body so well that it couldn't be found for thirty years, you would also have to accept the idea that she was capable of concealing the presence of someone else in the canyon.

"Did you ever talk to Sam Ogelthorpe?" she asked Nick.

"Sure."

"Do you believe he saw anyone?"

"Maybe, or maybe he was just seeking attention. Hard to tell with Sam. He produced a cow carcass, but he could have killed the cow himself. If he was telling the truth, then I'd be wrong about Jonathan dying in Slickrock Canyon. He could have died on Cedar Mesa, which would make the body just about impossible to find."

"Do you think Ogelthorpe could have killed him? It would have been a lot easier for him to hide the body than it would have been for Jennie Dell."

"That's something we may never know unless Sam confesses. I'll tell you one thing," Nick said. "I am convinced that Jonathan Vail is dead. Ada had unlimited funds, and I spent years looking for him. I searched Utah. I searched the Southwest. I went to Mexico. I went to Canada. Everywhere there was a sighting—and in the early years there were plenty of 'em—I went. Nothing ever checked out."

But was it in his interest that nothing ever checked out? Claire wondered. Searching the West—north and south—for

Jonathan Vail could be a lot more lucrative than doing background checks and conducting surveillance of unfaithful spouses, which is what his business was likely to consist of in Albuquerque.

"Did you ever feel you were getting close?" she asked.

"The only time I felt that was in San Miguel de Allende in Mexico. Beautiful place. Have you been there?"

"I have," Claire said. She knew it to be a charming town of cobblestone streets, pastel houses, and handcarved doorways. The market had the most beautifully arranged produce she'd ever seen. Even the street vendors were artists in San Miguel de Allende. It had a cosmopolitan population. In some ways it resembled Santa Fe, but to Claire it was more interesting. The weather was good and living was cheap. It wouldn't be a bad place to spend a winter—or a life.

"I spent more time down there than I did anywhere else," Nick said. "Several people contacted Ada in the seventies claiming they had seen Jonathan in San Miguel. That was when the book took off and his reputation spread. At that time vets could go to the Instituto de Allende on the GI Bill, and it became a haven for a certain type of vet. The American Legion post was a bunch of guys stoned on drugs. A kind of cult developed around Jonathan. At one time soldiers hated him for his antiwar views but later they began to see that he'd been right. When it came to draft dodgers, Mexico had a policy of taking the bribe and looking the other way. It was a place Jonathan might have ended up.

"The vets had a writers' group, and a couple of them told me that Jonathan came to their meetings, but they were so zonked out it was hard to know what they saw. My personal opinion was that it was someone passing as Jonathan. They told me the guy—whoever he was—got in a bar fight at La Cucaracha.

Some reports said he killed somebody, others said he got killed himself. In the seventies bodies weren't embalmed in Mexico. They had to be in the ground or out of the country in twenty-four hours. Whoever got killed in that fight was buried the same day in a pauper's grave with no identification. I checked it out. If you can't afford to go on paying for a grave the bones get dug up and dumped on the ground and the hole filled with someone else. It made it difficult to track down just who got killed. I didn't hear of any more Jonathan Vail sightings in San Miguel de Allende after that, but they slowed down everywhere in the late seventies. When amnesty was granted, I stopped searching. If Jonathan was alive at that point he would have come back."

"Did you ever come across a vet named Lou Bastiann in your investigation?"

"The Lou who is mentioned in the journal?"

"Yes."

Nick spun his chair. "I don't remember him but it's been a long time. I'd have to check my notes to be sure."

"Would you do that?"

"Sure," he said. "I had an index of everybody I talked to. Let me see if I can find it."

While he went to the back room to look, Claire examined the photos on his shelf. There was one of a young Nick with a crew cut wearing a police uniform. There were several of him at various stages of his life with different women. It depressed Claire that Nick, who remained short-legged and barrel-chested, kept showing up with younger women. One photograph that interested her was a man in bell bottoms with an unruly brown Afro as wide as the bottom of his pants. Would the hippie getup be considered shallow cover, she wondered, or deep? When Nick returned, she was holding that photo in her hand.

He laughed. "I was doing some surveillance in the sixties and went undercover as a hippie. Hard to believe I ever had that much hair, isn't it?"

"Were you ever a cop?" she asked.

"Yup. Five years with the APD. That's me in the uniform."

"The demonstration where you saw Jennie Dell—do you remember what band was playing?"

"It was a local band. I knew the drummer. They broke up soon after that demonstration. What was their name? The Margaritas—something like that."

"I was there," Claire said. "I was visiting a friend of mine at UNM. Who was it exactly you were surveilling?"

"I was following Jennie around to see if she would lead me to Jonathan."

"That demonstration took place in the summer of '66 before Jonathan disappeared. He participated in it. He sat on the podium with Jennie, and he spoke."

"Is that right?"

"It's right. I remember it well."

Nick was behind his desk again, spinning the back of his chair. Claire had him red-handed, and she hoped he would see that denial would be useless. He might even think it would be pointless, since the event in question had taken place over thirty years ago and would be remembered only by students who'd been in attendance. But to Claire, the archivist, what happened then would never be pointless.

Nick threw up his hands, laughed, and said, "You got me. Ada won't like me telling you this, but I don't want to lie to you, either. Truth is, I began tailing Jonathan from the time he got his draft notice. Ada was afraid he would split. My job was to prevent that from happening, or if I couldn't prevent it, to find

Ada's blue-eyed boy and bring him home. He never knew I was watching him. I was real careful."

Claire wondered whether the hippie clothes had provided any cover. There were people in the sixties who believed that once a cop, always a cop, and claimed they could spot one miles away. "If he didn't know he was being watched, then why hide out in a place as remote as Slickrock Canyon?" she asked.

"He liked remote places."

"Did you follow him there?" If he admitted it, the next question would be were you the hippie Sam Ogelthorpe saw?

Nick caught the spinning chair, held it in place, looked Claire right in the eye, and said, "Nope. Jonathan eluded me. I didn't go to Slickrock until after he disappeared."

But Claire was talking to a man who'd spent years concealing himself and his purpose. She shouldn't be surprised if he had learned to face people when he lied to them or to look away when he didn't. She was ready to go, but there was still the issue of the index. She reminded him of it.

"I couldn't find it, Nick said. "I must have put it in storage. I'll track it down and let you know. All right?"

"All right," Claire said.

He thanked her for her help. She thanked him for his. She got in her truck and drove back to the library, feeling that lies were buzzing at her like mosquitoes. Claire knew that history is revisionist. Other than dates and documents, there were few absolutes. The past was often a matter of perception. Even without deliberate distortion, people were capable of perceiving the same event differently. Still, when she put together all she once knew about Jonathan Vail and all she had learned, it was clear that someone was lying. The only inescapable conclusions were that he had died in the canyons, he had died somewhere else, or he hadn't. In a way it shouldn't matter to an archivist.

What mattered was that the legend survived. Legend rarely yielded to fact, and the mystery ensured this legend's survival. But the deeper Claire got into the mystery, the more important it became to discover the facts.

12

Chapter Twelve

"I've been meaning to thank you for your note. "It's been real hard to talk about Tim," Vivian Sansevera said when she called Claire back.

"I understand," Claire said.

"I'd like to meet you and visit the center. Tim spoke well of you and your work. I'm beginning to feel like getting out again. Maybe later in the week?"

"That would be fine," Claire replied. They arranged to meet at two on Friday. After she hung up, Claire tried to create an image of Vivian Sansevera. Her voice seemed dulled by grief, which Claire had expected. She'd been listening for an accent or phrase that would indicate whether Vivian was Anglo or Hispanic or Indian or where she was from. Her guess, from Vivian's lack of an accent, was California. In Claire's experience people who spoke unaccented English tended to be Californians. As to whether Vivian was Anglo or not, she couldn't say.

Shortly after two on Friday she received a call from the reception desk saying that Vivian Sansevera had arrived. Ruth O'Connor caught up with Claire on her way out, wanting to chat. Claire disengaged herself as soon as she was able, but by the time she got to the reception area Vivian Sansevera was not there.

"Where did she go?" she asked the grad student who manned the desk.

"Outside," the student replied.

Claire walked through the exhibition room and the lobby, went out the front door, and saw no one who seemed the right age to be Tim Sansevera's mother. There was a distinguished-looking Hispanic woman who appeared to be waiting for someone. Her thick black hair had turned silvery in front and framed her face like wings. She was an elegant woman, but closer to the age of Tim's grandmother than his mother. A small woman with a pale complexion and auburn hair sat on the steps smoking. She looked too young to be Tim's mother, but everyone else Claire saw was lugging the backpack of a student. She was considering approaching the older woman, when the redhead stood up, put out her cigarette, and said, "You're Claire?"

"Yes. Vivian?"

"I am." She took Claire's hand. Vivian wore a flowered dress and a pink cardigan sweater. She was a pretty woman, small as a child, who immediately evoked the impulse to shelter and protect. Her porcelain skin was a perfect complement to her auburn hair, which to Claire's experienced eye did not appear dyed. She had the fair skin that comes from the damp, gray climate of the British Isles. Claire tried to keep her disappointment in check. If this woman and Jonathan Vail had produced a son, he might have looked like Tim, but it was unlikely that his surname would be Sansevera. That Tim was Jonathan's son was a fantasy she shouldn't have entertained. If only it were true, however, this pleasant-looking woman might have some claim to the notebook instead of the intractable Ada Vail.

"Now please don't tell me I look too young to be Tim's mother," Vivian said. "I'm forty-six. I was sixteen when he was born."

"Now I know where Tim got his red hair," Claire said.

"He got it from me," Vivian agreed. "But in many ways he took after his father. Tim had my eyes, too, which means his father had to have green eyes somewhere in the family tree. Would you mind if we sat out here and talked? It's too nice to go in."

Claire suspected that Vivian wanted to stay outside so she could smoke. In her mind the woman was showing a reckless disregard for her beauty and her health. Nevertheless, Claire said, "I don't mind," and led Vivian around the corner to a shady bench.

When they sat down, Vivian pulled a cigarette out of a pack and lit up again. "It's hard for me to come here," she said. "Tim loved this place. He walked me through the library once, pointing out the architectural features that make it unique." Her pale eyes filled with tears. To Claire, grief was a deep pool and Vivian was swimming through the depths, struggling for air. No advantage in life could compensate a mother for the loss of a child. To a parent it was absolutely the worst thing that could ever happen.

"I'm so sorry," Claire said, touching her hand.

"Give me a minute," Vivian said. "I'll be all right." She

looked away and smoked silently. When she finished the cigarette, she tried again. "I get some relief from knowing that Tim was doing the work he loved."

"Coming across Jonathan Vail's journal in Sin Nombre Canyon was an incredible discovery. Tim's name will always be connected with it."

"Jonathan was his hero."

"Do you know why?"

"Part of it was the writing. Tim's dream was to be a writer."

"I didn't know that," Claire said.

"He was a good writer, I think, but Joe, his father, didn't approve. Joe grew up poor in LA. He was the first person in his family to get a degree. After he graduated from UCLA, he went to work for the federal government, and he's still there, in the Social Security Administration now. In Joe's family, no matter how much you hate the job, you stick it out for the pension. Finally you retire, get the pension, and in a few years you're dead. You don't go off into the wilderness, take risks, write novels. The reason Tim was in the Ph.D. program was because of his dad. His dad did approve of getting a Ph.-fucking-D. Joe's one wild moment was me. We met in high school, attracted by our differences, I guess. I got pregnant. In those days, when that happened you got married."

"Are you still married?" Claire asked.

"No. It didn't work out. I was too wild for Joe. We got divorced. Joe married a Hispanic woman his family approved of and had three kids. I moved to New Mexico with Tim. In his own way Joe has been a good dad, a lot stricter than me, but maybe Tim needed that."

"You kept Joe's name?"

"I did. It seemed easier when you're raising a kid to have the same name."

"Some people here have a fantasy that Tim was Jonathan Vail's son and he may have found the notebook in a family closet or garage. For years the rumors have persisted that Jonathan left an heir."

"If he did, it wasn't Tim," Vivian said. "Joe is Tim's dad. We were high school sweethearts when Jonathan Vail camped out in Slickrock Canyon. Joe came for the funeral. And today I didn't feel up to driving yet, so he brought me over here. He's coming back to pick me up. He'd like to meet you and see the notebook."

"Of course," Claire replied.

"There's no doubt in my mind that Tim found the notebook in Sin Nombre Canyon. After he gave it to you, he came over to my house and told me all about it. He was so excited about the find and was looking forward to going back for the duffel bag. He was sorry he wasn't able to bring it out; he really thought it would solve the mystery of Jonathan Vail." Vivian looked at Claire with hope in her eyes that solving the mystery of Jonathan might solve the mystery of her son. "Did it?"

"We didn't find the duffel bag. It wasn't in the cave that Curt Devereux and I explored. It's possible we went to the wrong cave, though. The rangers are searching."

"Tim told me it was to the west of the half-moon petroglyph just beyond the rock slide. He said Jonathan's initials were carved in the wall."

"That's where we went," Claire replied. "But the duffel bag wasn't there."

"Oh, God," Vivian said. Her hands trembled as she struggled to extricate another cigarette from the pack. "I'm afraid that something truly horrible happened to my son."

The only thing that could be more awful than death by accident would be death by intent, Claire thought.

"The ranger mentioned suicide, but Tim wouldn't have committed suicide under any circumstances, and certainly not when things were going so well." Vivian set down the pack of cigarettes and put her hand over Claire's. It resembled being clutched by the claw of a bird. "Did you see him?" Vivian asked.

"Yes," Claire admitted. "He was lying on the rocks when I got there. I said a prayer for him and closed his eyes."

"The ranger said he fell five hundred feet, most likely from the ledge outside the cave. Did it look to you like he fell, or was he . . ." As she struggled with the word, her hand dug deeper into Claire's. "Pushed?"

"I think the rangers would be far more qualified to establish that than I would."

"No," Vivian insisted. "No, they wouldn't. You knew Tim, and they didn't. You know—like I know—that if Tim said there was a duffel bag in the cave that had information about Jonathan Vail's disappearance, then it was there. Tim didn't fabricate. I think what happened was Tim found something in that bag. Someone didn't like what he found and pushed him over the ledge."

"Did Tim say anything to you about meeting anyone in the canyon?"

"He told me he was meeting you and Curt Devereux."

"Did he say when?"

"Just that it would be on the weekend. The rangers have only the physical evidence to go on, but you know the story of Jonathan Vail. You know who would have the motive to do something like this."

Claire's hand felt like a small animal in the grip of a fierce hawk. "I wish I did know," Claire said softly, "but I don't."

"Then find out for me, please," Vivian said, suddenly releasing Claire's hand. While Claire flexed it to see if it still functioned, Vivian buried her pack of cigarettes in her purse. "Here comes Joe," she whispered. "He hates it when I smoke."

It depressed Claire that years after a divorce, a woman would still care what her ex-husband thought. Joe walked up to the bench, and Vivian introduced them. He was a small, neat man with short black hair and tense eyes behind wire-rimmed glasses. Right away he struck Claire as a man a woman wouldn't want to cross. Vivian began to flutter in his presence, fiddling with a ruffle on her dress as she introduced Claire.

"It's a pleasure to meet you," Joe said, shaking Claire's hand. Although his expression was frigid, his manners were impeccable.

"Nice to meet you," Claire said.

"My son spoke often of his work here. He loved this place, and now I can see why. It is a magnificent building."

"I'd be happy to show it to you," Claire said.

"I'd like that," Joe replied.

"I'll wait out here," Vivian said. "I've already seen the building."

As they turned their backs to Vivian and walked toward the center, Claire was sure she was reaching into her purse for the pack of cigarettes. Sometimes she thought smokers were more attached to the ritual of smoking—opening the pack, taking out the cigarette, lighting it, and extinguishing the match—than they were to the smoking itself. It had to be comforting in times of stress.

As she walked Joe through the center, pointing out the high ceilings and the rows of corbels and vigas, he showed restrained admiration. When they got to the unfortunate murals that depicted white people with facial features and professional jobs and brown people with blank faces and menial jobs, he gave a short laugh. He stopped Claire before they went through the center's wrought-iron door and asked if they could talk for a minute. They sat down on the leather cushions of the Mission-style chairs.

Joe paused before he spoke. He was a reserved and proud man, and Claire could see that what he was about to reveal was hard for him. "My ex-wife likes drama. She wants to believe that Tim was murdered," he began. "Perhaps it makes it easier for her to accept his death. There's passion in murder. An accidental death is so meaningless. I imagine she has talked to you about this."

"She has."

"This is ridiculous, of course. I would be grateful if you would pay no attention to her. I can think of no reason why anyone would want to murder Tim."

Claire could think of reasons. She could also understand why Vivian would want to believe Tim was murdered and Joe would not. In Joe's eyes, a murder might turn Tim into an unfortunate or an outlaw, and he would prefer to remember his son as a success. Claire evaded the issue by saying, "Tim did excellent work here. You should be very proud of him."

A light came on in Joe's sad eyes. "I was," he said "Very proud."

"Would you like to see the journal Tim found?"

"I would."

"I'll get Vivian," Claire said, leaving Joe alone for a minute while she went outside. When she and Vivian returned, she walked the two of them down the hallway, imagining how horrible it would be if she and Evan ever had to reunite around the death of a child. She got the briefcase from the safe and let Vivian and Joe look at it with white-gloved fingers in her office. Vivian read through the journal, seemingly enthralled by every word. Joe appeared bothered by the dirtiness of the briefcase and uninterested in the content of the journal. His repeated glances at his watch only increased Vivian's interest.

"Really, Vivian," he said finally. "We shouldn't take any more of Claire's time."

"Don't rush me," she snapped. "You're always rushing me."

"I am not always rushing you. We haven't even been married for twenty-five years."

"In a minute," Vivian said.

Joe went back to furtively glancing at his watch.

"Oh, all right," Vivian said, making a show of standing up and adjusting the ruffles on her dress. "Let's go."

"Thank you for your time," Joe said to Claire.

"I was glad to help," Claire said.

Vivian clutched her hand. "Let me know, please, please, please, if you find out anything."

"I will," Claire said.

She stood in her door and watched them walk down the hallway, thinking how some people's looks shaped their lives. Since Vivian, even at forty-six, looked like a child, people were inclined to treat her like one. Claire wondered if her youthful beauty had become a burden and if she smoked to make herself look older. Smoking was a reckless act. Recklessness was one trait Tim and his mother had in common. He had showed little of his father's respectful wariness, making Claire wonder if Joe didn't feel out of the loop. Even in her grief Vivian stepped lightly down the hallway, while Joe's motions were tight and economical. Claire wondered which of them was right about Tim's death. And what did she herself believe? Was it murder or an accident? Should she be investigating or should she leave it to the rangers? Were they doing anything?

She called Ellen Frank to find out. "I've just had a visit from Vivian Sansevera."

"How is she doing?" Ellen asked.

"Getting by. She's upset that you would consider Tim's death a suicide."

"We do have to explore every option," Ellen replied.

"Tim told Vivian he found the duffel bag."

"We searched Sin Nombre thoroughly, but still haven't found it. Our archeologist examined the cave, and she believes the Jonathan Vail initials are authentic. He was in that cave. He may well have left a duffel bag behind. Someone else may well have removed it, but we'll keep looking. It's unfortunate that Curt didn't get there sooner."

"The center's handwriting expert has authenticated the journal," Claire reported, "and we now know that the briefcase it was in came from Vietnam. It was sent to Jonathan by Lou Bastiann, the fan who is mentioned in the journal."

"The autopsy and the drug screen on Tim Sansevera came back," continued Ellen. "I'll give Vivian a call about it. There were no drugs in his system. He had numerous broken bones and the massive internal injuries consistent with a long fall. Death was caused by impact. The medical examiner couldn't establish the exact time of death, but it did happen the day you found him."

"Could he have been pushed?"

"There's no evidence of that."

Claire felt a duty to persevere, for the sake of Vivian Sansevera, for the legend of Jonathan Vail, for her own sake. "He might have met someone in the cave by arrangement or by accident. They fought over the duffel bag, and Tim got pushed off the ledge."

"I can understand how people who are in the Jonathan Vail business might want to believe in a conspiracy and to find a connection between the deaths," Ellen replied. "It's weird that

Tim would die in the same place where his hero is believed to have died and possibly even in the same way. It might indicate murder. But it could also indicate carelessness, which we see often enough in Grand Gulch. We'll go on looking, but until we find evidence of a crime, I can't involve the FBI."

"Are you checking alibis? There are people who might have found the contents of the duffel bag incriminating."

"Such as?"

"Jennie Dell. She knew that Tim had reported seeing it."

"Curt Devereux talked to her. She claims she was at home writing the day Tim died, although her only witness is her cat."

"There's Nick Lorenz, the private investigator Ada Vail hired to look for her son. She told him about the duffel bag."

"What possible motive would he have?"

"He admitted to me that he was tailing Jonathan in 1966 before he vanished. He might have followed him into Slickrock and been responsible for his death in some way." Claire was aware that she was moving out of the black-and-white world of historical fact and into the speculative realm of fiction.

"I'll look into it," Ellen said.

"There's also Curt Devereux. He was coming out of the canyon when I met him. He told me he had breakfast at the Navajo Cafe in Bluff, which should be easy enough to substantiate."

Ellen hesitated, and Claire wondered what she was doing. Staring out the window? Playing with her hair? Considering the fact that Curt was her superior in age and position? "Curt is the investigator on the Vail case," Ellen said carefully. "I am not in a position to investigate him. But . . ." She paused again, leaving Claire time to consider whether she was in a position to investigate Curt. "I'll let you know if anything new develops," Ellen said, indicating that the conversation was over.

"I'd appreciate that."

Staring out her own office window gave Claire a view of the hallway and her coworkers passing by, so she turned to the screen saver on her computer monitor for diversion. As *Portrait of a Lady* and *Huckleberry Finn* sprouted wings and flew off the shelves, she thought about her own work, which involved tracking down rare documents, checking facts, comparing handwriting, searching the Internet. It was a form of investigation that usually meant following a paper or database trail. Claire's work rarely poked into the lives of the living. Did she have any right to investigate them? she asked herself. How would the suspects feel about her questioning their motives and their lives? Would Ellen Frank object, or could the pause in her conversation be considered a sign of encouragement? If Jonathan and/or Tim had been murdered, the murderer could strike again. Knowing that and remembering the fierceness of Vivian Sansevera's grip were enough to involve Claire emotionally, but mentally she wondered whether she had anything to add to the investigation. Her professional knowledge of Jonathan's work could be an advantage, and her amateur status could allow her to follow hunches, while Ellen Frank needed evidence to proceed. Getting involved could put Claire at risk. But she might know enough to already be at risk, and Ellen Frank didn't appear to be taking any steps to lessen the odds. When it came to investments, Claire knew that risk had to be balanced against return. The same could be said of this investigation. The return could be enormous, not in money but in prestige and satisfaction. To Claire the best return of all would be solving the puzzle and setting things right. On the other hand, the risks were also enormous, extending possibly to her own safety. Her children were grown and on their own, but she was still a mother. Nevertheless, a question had been posed that she felt she could answer. If she proceeded, she would have to do it subtly and carefully, but that was how she did everything.

Claire began by thinking through whom she suspected and what she knew. She hadn't mentioned Lou Bastiann as a suspect to Ellen Frank. If Ellen thought Nick Lorenz was far-fetched, she would have to think Lou was out of the ballpark. He was said to be in Vietnam at the time of Jonathan's disappearance, a fact that should be easy enough to check. Besides, what motive would a devoted fan have for killing his hero? And Lou was presumably in Missouri at the time of Tim's death, although Claire had no way of confirming that.

Curt and Nick had possible motives, and their guilt or innocence could rest on their alibis. She put them on hold for a moment and turned her thoughts to Jennie Dell, the lover and the fiction writer. Her appeal to men was obvious, but what kind of a writer was she? A novel set in the Southwest ought to be on the center's shelves, yet when she searched the database for Jennie Dell nothing came up.

She decided to call Jennie. "Hey," Jennie said when Claire identified herself. "I've been intending to call you."

"What about?"

"I talked to Lou Bastiann. He's bothered about Ada's plans for the journal. We all agree that Jonathan's work should be published exactly as is."

"I wish it were our decision to make."

"I called Ada," Jennie whispered in her husky voice, "and set up a meeting with Lou and me. She wouldn't do it just for me, but she's always receptive to flattery from a fan. Would you like to come? Maybe the three of us can change her mind."

"She seems determined."

"True, but we have to try, don't we? If Jonathan were here, it would break his heart to see his journal cut to bits."

"Should I let Ada know that I will be coming, too?"

"I'll tell her," Jennie said.

"When are you meeting?"

"Tuesday at three-thirty at her house."

"All right. If Ada has no objection, I'll be there."

"Thank you so much," Jennie sighed. "Now, why was it you called me?"

"I wanted to read your novel, but I couldn't find it in the center's database."

"It had a very small print run. Still, you ought to have a copy. I'll bring one with me on Tuesday."

"Good," Claire replied.

"I'll call if Ada objects to your coming. Otherwise we'll see you at her house."

Claire decided she would tell Harrison about the meeting with Ada after the fact. There was always the possibility that he would discourage her or would want to come himself, which could make a tricky negotiation impossible. Harrison had a way of hardening people's attitudes.

13

Chapter Thirteen

Since Jennie never called back, Claire assumed the meeting was on. She left the library at three on Tuesday afternoon. On the drive to Ada's she thought about Lou and Jennie, wondering how often they saw each other and what kind of relationship they had. She arrived at the Vails' typically early, at three-twenty, and saw Jennie's green Honda and Lou's motorcycle with Missouri plates already parked beside the curb. When she rang the doorbell, the maid answered, looking straight at Claire's face and smiling, in contrast to her previously diffident manner.

"They are in the living room," she said, turning and padding down the hallway.

Claire followed, preparing herself to face Ada, doubting it would be possible for even the most devoted or obsequious fan to change her mind. Charm might accomplish what reason couldn't, but she hadn't seen much charm in Lou Bastiann. He sat on a white sofa with his back to the door, leaning toward Otto, who was in his usual place in his wheelchair. Lou held his sunglasses in one hand and gestured with them as he talked. Otto's faded eyes were riveted on him and didn't move when Claire entered the room. Jennie stood behind Otto, gently massaging his shoulders.

"Claire," she said. "We're so glad you could come."

"Hey," said Lou, putting on his sunglasses and turning to face Claire. The light was bright in Ada's living room, and Claire hadn't taken her own sunglasses off yet, although she intended to do so, as a sign of respect for Otto.

A lawnmower droned in the backyard. Ada was not in the room. Claire had the sense that every piece of furniture was exactly where it had been on her previous visit, yet Ada's absence created a disturbance and a void, making her feel that it would be better not to step any farther into the room. She paused at the first sofa and asked, "Where is Ada?"

"Something came up, and she had to cancel at the last minute." Jennie smiled. Her cheeks were flushed. She wore a plum-colored dress with long, full sleeves. "Isn't that right, Esperanza?" she asked the maid.

"*Sí*," the maid answered.

"And the nurse?" Claire asked.

"It's her day off," Jennie said.

"I don't think we should be meeting without Ada."

"Oh, she wouldn't mind," Jennie said with a careless wave of her hand. "I left Madrid early. She probably called after I left, and I didn't know not to come. Since I was here already, I just thought I'd say hello to Otto and introduce Lou. A lot of fans have been to see Ada, but Otto gets to see so very few."

Once again Claire wondered what Otto saw. Although his eyes were focused on Lou, his expression was blank.

"Come in," Jennie coaxed with a seductive smile. "Otto would like to see you, too. He sees well up close, but not across the room."

Claire doubted that, remembering how Otto's eyes had followed her to the painting above the mantel. The lawn mower hiccuped and resumed its steady drone. The signals were strong that this meeting was a sham: the vehicles parked outside before the appointed hour, the smile on the maid's face that might have been induced by money in her pocket, the fact that it was the nurse's day off and that Jennie could well have known that Ada had another event scheduled for this day and this time. If this assumption were correct, and Ada found out a meeting had been held behind her back, she would be furious and could cause Claire considerable trouble. Yet she found herself being drawn into the room, passing the first seating arrangement and approaching the one that included Otto.

"Do you remember Claire Reynier, Otto?" Jennie asked him.

At least she didn't yell at him as if she were talking to a stupid child, Claire thought. She was beside the wheelchair now, and she removed her sunglasses. "Hello, Otto," she said, bending down and touching the back of his wrinkled hand. Otto's eyes remained focused on Lou Bastiann, but there was no indication that his brain registered what they saw. Lou could have been a person, a knickknack, or a piece of furniture.

He leaned back into the sofa, crossed his arms, and watched Otto. He wore the same black jeans, black T-shirt, and boots that he'd worn the day Claire met him. With his muscular arms and callused hands, he was a rough edge, a burr in the polished living room. Claire had the sensation that when he stood up he would leave a stain on the white sofa.

"Let's tell Otto about the journal," Jennie said, sitting down on the sofa beside Lou.

"He already knows," Claire said, in consideration of the fact that Otto's brain might still be working.

"I'll remind him," Jennie said. "Otto, Jonathan's journal was found in Sin Nombre Canyon, the journal that has been missing for so many years." Otto gave no response. Claire knew this conversation should not be taking place, but she was too fascinated to pull herself away.

"The University of New Mexico Press wants to publish the journal," Jennie continued, "but Ada intends to edit it and cut the heart out of the book. She wants to take out the anger and the passion that made Jonathan's voice unique. She intends to silence him and turn him into her good son. You know that wasn't Jonathan. He was a protester, an activist. "How do you feel, Otto? We"—she looked to Lou and Claire for confirmation—"believe the journal should be published exactly as it is. Can you find a way to tell us what you feel, Otto?"

Lou's rough hand rested on top of Otto's, which was pale and soft and dappled with age spots. The old man's eyes seemed to be losing definition, giving Claire the sensation she had when looking at La Sagrada Familia or at the walls of Slickrock Canyon from the helicopter, that reality was segueing into hallucination. They filled as slowly and gently as a depression in sodden ground, when the last drop of rain was one too many. As Otto's eyes filled, his lips moved, though not a word came out. Eventually his eyes overflowed and a teardrop fell onto his wrist. How terrible, thought Claire, to be able to cry but not to wipe the tears away.

Lou lifted his bandanna and gently dabbed Otto's eyes. "It's okay, old man," he said. "It's okay."

"He does understand," Jennie crowed. "The one way he can

communicate is through tears, but he is capable of telling us what he wants."

It was a moving demonstration, but even if Otto had said in a loud, clear voice that he did not want to see Jonathan's journal edited, even if he had written a note in his own hand, Claire didn't know what she could do about it. The decision of how to publish the journal was in the hands of Harrison and the UNM Press committee. Claire certainly didn't want to discuss the possibilities in front of Otto and reduce him to a deaf-and-dumb statue again. "We should go," she said. "Otto is getting tired. We've violated his privacy enough."

"Of course," Jennie said. "We don't want to wear him out." She stood up, bent over Otto and gave him a hug, letting her long blond hair fall across his shoulders. "Thank you so much, Otto. We'll do all we can. Our thoughts will be with you."

"Take care," Lou said, giving Otto's hand a final squeeze. He stood up, leaving not a stain but an imprint on the white sofa.

The maid led the way down the hall, closing the front door after the visitors as they left the house. Claire heard the tap of Lou's boots behind her on the sidewalk. The sun lit up a cottonwood tree across the street, turning the leaves to gold. She felt she'd been duped, and her anger burned. When they reached the street, she turned to face Jennie and Lou.

Before she could speak, Lou glanced at the cottonwood leaves and said, "They look like pieces of eight."

Jennie laughed. It was the first time Claire had seen any real interaction between her and Lou. Her laughter had a scornful edge. "The old pirate metaphor," she said.

Claire had more on her mind than metaphors. "You set up that meeting without ever talking to Ada. You knew she would be gone this afternoon," she accused Jennie.

"Oh, come on," Jennie replied, tossing her head and flipping her hair across her shoulder. "You're an intelligent woman. You must have known what I was up to. Did you really believe Ada would let us in to see Otto?"

"You told me we were going to see Ada."

"Did I?" Jennie asked.

"If Ada finds out we were here, she could cause me a lot of trouble."

"She won't find out unless we stand out here discussing it and waxing poetic about the cottonwood trees until she comes home."

Lou seemed embarrassed and stared at his boots, but Claire persevered. "You lied to me," she insisted. Once a person is discovered in a lie, her words form a continuous loop, with no telling when the lies began or when they will end. Everything Jennie had ever said had become suspect in Claire's mind. She didn't enjoy standing in the street arguing, but she was too angry to just walk away.

"Could we call it a misunderstanding?" Lou asked in the tone of a man who believes he's being confronted by the irrationality of women. His face, behind the dark glasses, was almost as blank as Otto's. His coolness annoyed Claire. She wanted to take him by the shoulders and shake some expression into him.

"I'm sorry you feel that way," Jennie said. Her voice was frigid, but she hadn't fulfilled her purpose yet, and she reached deep in her throat and pulled up some of the warmth she had previously demonstrated for Claire. "You saw how sad Otto was," she said. "You saw his tears. He doesn't want the journal to be cut any more than we do."

"Otto has a lot to be sad about," Claire replied. "I can't assume his tears were over the journal, and even if I did I don't know what I could do about it."

"Stop Ada from being the editor," Jennie pleaded.

"You're overestimating the power I have at UNM."

Jennie lifted her dark glasses and fixed icy blue eyes on Claire. "People have the power they choose to have. People have the power they assume."

People who are willing to lie about their actions do, thought Claire. They have the power to commit crimes, to conceal crimes, and to wreck other people's lives. She wanted to get away from Jennie Dell, but she had one more question. "Did you bring your book with you?"

"So sorry, I forgot."

"What is the title?"

"*Out of the Blue*." Jennie looked back at the house. Claire followed her gaze and saw the drapes in the window slide shut. "We have to go," Jennie said, suggesting she had received a signal. The one signal that would be relevant at this point was that Ada was coming home.

Fearing that this might be her last chance to talk to Lou, Claire took a business card from her purse.

"Would you please call me?" she asked. "There are things I need to talk to you about."

Lou slid the card into the pocket of his jeans and said, "Sure," but his offhand manner made Claire doubt she would ever see or hear from him again.

They went to their respective vehicles and drove away. Claire avoided Central, thinking that if Ada were on her way home, that was the way she would drive in. She knew that if Harrison had been a witness to the meeting, he'd have insisted that she wait for Ada and tell her exactly what had transpired inside her house. Usually when Harrison suggested something, that was reason enough not to do it. In this case Claire's conscience told her that Harrison was right, but if Ada found out about the meeting, she might be far too angry to allow the journal to remain at the center or to be published by UNM Press. Claire felt that as Jonathan's archivist, her first loyalty was to the integrity of his journal. As an administrator, Harrison had other agendas. It didn't entirely resolve the issue, but it allowed Claire to put it on the shelf for the time being and replay the afternoon in her mind. The meeting had revealed a tension between Jennie and Lou that Claire didn't know enough about either of them to explain. It had demonstrated that Otto wasn't entirely deaf and dumb, that he had awareness and feelings, although it did not make clear exactly what his feelings were. To live like Otto was the worst fate Claire could imagine. Far better, in her mind, to be dead.

She wondered if Jennie had a purpose for arranging the meeting that had not been revealed yet. The integrity of Jennie Dell, which had long been in doubt, had finally been proved to be nonexistent. Her actions today cast doubt on all her previous actions. Claire wanted to read her book, not because she expected a novel to reveal the truth about an author but because she was curious abut the quality of Jennie's writing.

When she got back to the library she searched the title index on her computer and found two books titled *Out of the Blue*, neither of which had been written by Jennie Dell, although both were published in the mid-seventies, about the time when Jennie might have written her novel. One of them was by a mystery writer whose work Claire knew and admired, and the other was nonfiction. Considering that Jennie's statement that her book was a work of fiction could also be a fiction, Claire went looking for the nonfiction book on the shelves in Zimmerman and found an account of sailing solo across the Atlantic, with a picture of the male author in his sailboat on the jacket flap.

She went back to her office, logged on to Amazon.com and ran a title search for *Out of the Blue*. Amazon had a database of more than four million titles and appeared to list every book that had ever been in print on any subject. *Out of the Blue* was a ubiquitous title that turned up several times in a decade. Claire found the two she had already discovered, another *Out of the Blue* in 1963, one more in 1970, and two in 1975. Amazon gave little information about books that had long been out of print, but enough for Claire to establish that none of the books titled *Out of the Blue* had been written by Jennie Dell. Had her tale about the novel been a fabrication, too? A distortion of the facts? A half-truth? The only way to find out would be to get the books. Next, she did an author search on Jennie Dell and came across the mini books but no novel. There were five mini books in print on various subjects. Their sales ranking ranged from 150,000 to 200,000. Claire knew she could find these near the checkout counter at local bookstores. Amazon would be willing to locate the out-of-print *Out of the Blue*'s for her, but John Harlan, with all his connections, could do it faster and cheaper.

On her way home from work Claire stopped at Page One. They had two of Jennie's mini books, one on astrology and one on dogs. She bought both of them and drove across Juan Tabo to Page One, Too, the used-books store, where she found John Harlan sitting with his feet up talking on the phone.

He bid good-bye to the person he was speaking to, then said, "I've been wondering how you were."

"All right," Claire said. "Except that I've been getting the run-around from Jennie Dell."

"Hell," John replied, "she's been giving people the run-around all her life, hasn't she? She ought to be pretty good at it by now. She was of that 'if it feels good, do it' hippie era. Some of those hippies were capable of rationalizing just about anything they wanted to do. For all the talk about peace and love, they practiced a lot of deception and manipulation. I was married and runnin' the family business in the sixties myself. I didn't have time for sex, drugs, and rock and roll, did you?"

"Not to the extent that Jennie Dell did. She told me the name of her novel is *Out of the Blue*."

"When was it published?"

"She didn't say. I found several books with that title on Amazon.com, but none of them in her name."

"Maybe she used a pseudonym."

"Maybe so, Claire said. "I made a list of all the *Out of the Blue*s that were published in the sixties and seventies, including the name of the author and the publisher. Could you find me copies?"

"Sure," John said, putting his feet on the floor and looking at the list. "Price is no object?"

"It might be," Claire said. "But if it is an expensive book you or I would have heard of it, wouldn't we?"

"If it's set in the Southwest, we would. Was it?"

"I thought so, but now I'm not so sure."

"Why not call Jennie and ask her?"

"I don't want to talk to Jennie. At this point, I wouldn't believe a word she says."

"You doing anything for dinner?" John asked.

"No." Claire knew that her datura only had a few flowers left. If she intended to invite John over to share the blossoming, it would have to be now or not until spring. She hesitated briefly, then decided against it. Her energy had been drained by the duplicity of the meeting this afternoon. "How about Chow's?" she asked.

"That's the place that puts pesto on their dumplings?"

"They're called pot stickers," Claire corrected him.

"Whatever you call 'em, it's a piece of dough stuffed with something, right?"

"You could say that," Claire replied, wondering what she could possibly serve John if she ever did invite him for dinner.

"Could I get something simple there like wonton soup or egg rolls?" John asked.

"You could," Claire said. But why would anybody want to? she asked herself.

John stood up and grabbed his jacket from the back of a chair. "Let's do it," he said.

Claire had the pot stickers with cilantro pesto, a delicious mix of China and the Southwest. John stuck with egg rolls and wonton soup. When the cottonwoods turned gold, the nights turned cool, and Claire smelled woodsmoke in the air as they left the restaurant.

When she got home, she climbed into bed with Nemesis and Jennie's mini books. She clicked the remote and the fake log in her gas fireplace burst into real flame. Although the books were on subjects in which she had no particular interest, the writing was clean and better than she would have expected in this particular format. With a sales ranking of 150,000 to 200,000 and a price of five dollars a book, she supposed a woman could make a living at it if she drove old cars, wore old clothes, and lived in Madrid in a house that was paid for.

14

Chapter Fourteen

When Nick Lorenz called, Claire's first reaction was guilt. The thought crossed her mind that Ada had found out she was at her house and hired him to investigate. She was relieved when he told her he'd found the missing files from the Jonathan Vail investigation.

"They were in my garage," he said. "I moved them out a couple of years ago when the office was getting too cluttered. I met Lou Bastiann in San Miguel de Allende. Once I looked at the file I remembered him. I just didn't remember his name. After twenty years, names tend to go. I'll show you my notes if you'd like to get together."

"How about after work?" Claire asked. "Around six?"

"That would be fine. Let's meet at my office."

"See you then," Claire replied.

Harrison spent the day pacing up and down the hall, casting his shadow before him. Every time he passed Claire's office, she waited for him to stop and chastise her for the visit to Otto Vail, but he never did.

After work she drove across town to Nick's mall. It was the time just before nightfall that was known as civil twilight, a phrase Claire loved. It was a golden hour at a golden time of year. In the valley the cottonwoods were radiant in the light. In New Mexico myth didn't yield to fact, and beauty didn't yield to metaphor. There was nothing the light here could be compared to, Claire thought. It was the standard by which all light should be measured. On her last trip to Nick's office, she had noticed a datura beside Osuna laden with spent blossoms. Today there were none. The valley was starting to have frosts at night, and the season had ended.

She parked near Nick's office, got out of her car, and looked at the Sandias, which were reflecting the sunset's afterglow, turning the color of sangria silhouetted against a pale blue sky. It was a view that Claire preferred to the long western view from her house in the heights. She stopped to savor the colors and the moment. She should be knocking on Nick Lorenz's door, but the afterglow was brief and she waited until the sun sank lower in the sky and the mountains lost their radiance. A Toyota pickup with a balloon plate was parked directly in front of Nick's suite, and she assumed it belonged to him. When she knocked at the door, Nick answered so quickly she would have sworn he'd been standing behind it waiting for her summons. He wore a white shirt open at the neck to show off his gold chains. The shag carpeting and fake wood paneling in his office were even more tacky under the fluorescent lighting. The ugliness of his office was a sharp contrast to the beauty of the sunset, but it was a contrast that Claire experienced often enough in Albuquerque, a city that encompassed both the hideous and the sublime.

"How ya doin'?" Nick asked.

"All right. And you?"

"Not too shabby."

"Have you talked to Ada recently?"

"Not since I saw you last. Come in. I'll show you the file."

A fat manila folder lay on his desk. Claire sat down in the office chair, glancing again at the photographs on the shelf behind Nick. In some ways he was a master of disguise—crew cuts, Afros; khakis, bell bottoms; gold chains, love beads. The PI who could blend into any crowd. But the one thing he could never disguise was his lack of height and his chunky build. She noticed that in all of Nick's incarnations his weight and shape varied very little.

He opened the file and said, "Thank God for notes. I talked to so many people during this investigation, sometimes it was hard to keep them straight. Here's a description I wrote up of Lou."

He handed Claire a piece of yellow lined paper, its rough edge indicating that it had been ripped from a pad. His handwriting was distinctive, but borderline legible, resembling chicken scratches in the dust. It wouldn't be hard to establish that this was Nick's writing, but dating it would be more complicated. The paper and the ink looked old, but twenty years old? Claire couldn't say. She was able to decipher the following description: "medium sized, brown-haired guy, dark eyes, scar on chin, quiet, serious way of talking. Limp on left leg. A vet."

"Is that the guy you know?" Nick asked.

"It could be. Lou is medium-sized. His eyes are dark. He limps with his left leg. The brown hair could have turned gray by now. His beard could be hiding the scar on his chin. What was he doing in San Miguel de Allende? Did he tell you?"

"I didn't ask. I assumed it was what all the other vets were doing: hanging out in La Cucaracha, getting stoned, taking courses at the Instituto so he could stay on the GI Bill."

"Did he say anything about Jonathan?"

"He was one of the guys who told me that Jonathan was killed in the bar fight at La Cucaracha. I heard that from a couple of people."

Claire remembered La Cucaracha as a seedy bar near the *jardín*, where the more rowdy members of the expatriate community hung out. "You're sure he said he was killed in La Cucaracha," she asked, "and not somewhere else?" But where else, she thought to herself, if not Sin Nombre Canyon?

"That's what he said. See?" He showed Claire a scratchy note that read, "Lew Bestin says Jonathan killed in fight in La Cucaracha."

Claire studied the note, which was written with a black ball-point pen on yellow lined paper just like the description was. Were they the same vintage? Without a detailed analysis it would be difficult to say. "Why didn't Lou tell me that? Why didn't he tell the family?" she asked.

"He could have been the killer. He looked like a guy who'd been in a few scrapes, a guy who had a mean streak."

"You think Lou Bastiann would have killed his hero?"

Nick grinned at her from across the desk, showing teeth that were filled with gold, Ada's gold. "People kill their heroes all the time. That's what myths are all about, isn't it? Slaying the father, the monster, the hero?"

"I find it hard to believe," Claire said.

"I did, too, to tell you the truth. Not that Lou Bastiann killed somebody, but that the somebody who got killed was

Jonathan. He was idolized in that little town. If he was killed in San Miguel de Allende, more people would have known about it. The body would have been sent back to this country, not thrown in a pauper's grave within twenty-four hours. I had the money to pay anyone who could substantiate that story, but no one ever did. Someone got killed in La Cucaracha, someone got buried, but I don't think the someone was Jonathan Vail. I think Lou told me that because he wanted me to stop searching and get out of town."

"Why did he care whether or not you stopped searching?"

"Why do you care about preserving the memory of Jonathan Vail? He had been gone ten years by then and was already a legend. People get attached to their legends and want to hang on to them. It's easier to deal with them than with real people, no? Lou was interested in preserving the legend. I was interested in locating a person."

"Once a legend gets established, it becomes difficult, if not impossible, to disprove it."

"True."

"Did you tell Curt Devereux what you found in San Miguel de Allende?"

"What was there to tell? All I found was smoke and mirrors. Ada didn't want me talking to Devereux about my investigation. If I'd come across anything tangible, I would have had to report it, but that never happened."

"The center would love to have your notes and an account of your search for Jonathan Vail." As Claire said these words, the disadvantage of being an amateur investigator became clear. She could only ask that Nick give her his notes; Ellen Frank had the power to subpoena them.

"I'd have to run that by Ada, of course."

"Of course. By now you've probably spent more time

looking for Jonathan than he spent living."

"The search became greater than the man, and the legend more interesting than Jonathan ever was. In my opinion he was outspoken but weak. He talked a lot about rebellion, but he was really talking about rebelling against his mother. If he'd lived longer, he might have broken away from her and become his own person, but I never saw that happen. I think that for him running away from the draft would have had more to do with fear than principle."

"He wrote a book that became a classic and influenced a lot of people."

Nick leaned back in his chair. "Well, I'm not a librarian or an author myself, but it seems to me that character has little do to with writing ability."

"You could be right," Claire said.

"Would you like me to make you copies of the Lou Bastiann notes?"

"Please."

He ran off the copies on his photocopier and handed them to Claire. Copies weren't as revealing as the originals, but they were better than nothing.

"Can you tell me anything else about Lou?" she asked.

"Only that he seemed lost to me, but many people in San Miguel de Allende did, especially the vets. Vietnam left people adrift. Nothing in life was ever as challenging or as interesting again."

Claire stood up and shook his hand. "Thank you for your help," she said.

"My pleasure," Nick replied.

She went outside to the parking lot, which was dark and nearly empty at this end of the mall, although several cars were parked in front of a Korean restaurant at the other end. Lights were visible on top of the Sandias, but otherwise the mountains had blended into the night. Claire got into her truck, drove to the Korean restaurant, and parked beside the cars that were already there. While she waited, she wondered if Nick had told her the truth about San Miguel de Allende. It had to be one of the more charming places he visited during his investigation of Jonathan Vail. What was to stop him from inventing a near miss and a false death to keep the investigation alive? It would keep him in San Miguel de Allende and keep the checks coming. He wasn't aware that Claire didn't know how to contact Lou. In fact, if she really tried, she probably could find him and check his word against Nick's. What if their stories didn't coincide? Suppose Lou said he had never met Nick, had never been to San Miguel de Allende, had never told him Jonathan was killed in a bar fight? If it turned out to be Nick's word and his sketchy notes against Lou's word twenty years later, Claire wondered whom she would believe. That Nick's description had been reasonably accurate was a mark in his favor.

She could see his office door from where she sat, and her thoughts were interrupted when he came outside and got in his pickup. He turned on the lights, started the engine, and drove out of the parking lot, with Claire behind him. Her Chevy pickup was as generic in appearance as his Toyota, so she doubted he would notice her if he happened to turn around. She had never followed anyone before—not even her ex-husband when he was cheating on her—but the key had to be staying close enough to keep the other vehicle in sight and far enough back to remain unnoticed. She let a couple of cars get between them, hoping not to lose him at a light. Nick turned south on Fourth Street and west on Montaño, which didn't surprise her. He was likely to be headed home, and Montaño would take him across the river to the West Side.

Although Montaño was wide enough for two lanes in each direction, only one was permitted, as a concession to the people who lived near the bridge in the North Valley. Two cars were between Claire and Nick's pickup, but she was able to keep him in sight as he crossed the bridge and continued west on Montaño. The cars eventually turned in at various subdivisions and Claire had to drop back to maintain an inconspicuous distance. The streetlights were bright enough that Nick would see her truck if he turned around. She could clearly see the vehicle behind her in her rearview mirror. On the other hand, Nick had no reason to look behind him, and even if he did, he might not have noticed what kind of vehicle Claire drove, unless he'd had her under surveillance, too.

He turned off into a subdivision where the streets were named after historical battles, an irony that amused Claire. The turns came more quickly here, and she had to close in so she didn't lose him at Appomattox or Wounded Knee. This was a middle-class neighborhood where all the houses had garages out front and were so identical that if a property owner came home under the influence, she could easily end up at the wrong door. Ada's money hadn't brought her son back, and it hadn't brought Nick wealth either. He made a quick right onto Glorieta, and his brake lights came on. Either he'd spotted Claire or he'd arrived at his house. She stayed on Gettysburg and took the next right, hoping she could circle around and catch up to him from the other side as he pulled into his garage. Some of the streets here were cul-de-sacs. If she ended up in one of those, it would bring her investigation to a standstill.

She made two more right-hand turns and found herself coming at Nick on Glorieta from the opposite direction, just as she had hoped. His garage door was open and he was driving inside. A woman stood in the light of the house's front door apparently waiting for him. Claire gave her a quick glance and saw that she wore skintight pants and appeared to be considerably younger than Nick. How did he do it? she wondered before turning her attention to Nick's two-car garage. The light was on, and she could see that the other space was taken by a subcompact. It was all Claire needed to know. She kept going while Nick parked his pickup. She hadn't learned the make or model of the subcompact, but she'd learned that the other car in Nick's garage wasn't a white Dodge van. Not to say he couldn't have borrowed one somewhere. She'd already ruled the van out as too old to be a rental. It didn't prove Nick wasn't at Slickrock when Tim was killed, but it lowered the odds that he had been there.

Driving back across the bridge, Claire thought about the surveillance she'd just conducted. Her first attempt had been rather successful. She'd discovered what she wanted to discover. She didn't believe she'd been noticed. She hadn't spent hours of total boredom trying not to pee. Was this a job she would ever consider if things didn't work out at UNM? The answer was no. She loved her work at the center, and although she didn't mind poking into the lives of the dead, she disliked disturbing the privacy of the living.

In the morning Claire practiced tai chi, trying to keep her mind free of plans and questions and thoughts. The one thought that pestered her like an annoying fly was that she should call Curt Devereux. She imagined herself putting a glass jar over the fly and the thought, taking it to the window and releasing it, being determined to think about Curt later, over coffee. Claire finished with the infinite ultimate stance, took a shower, made a cup of coffee, and sat down in the window overlooking her courtyard. There was no denying that her datura had ceased to bloom. It had no buds, and the pods had burst and dropped their seeds all over the brick floor of the courtyard.

Her reason for calling Curt was to see if he had heard any rumors of Jonathan being in San Miguel de Allende. The problem was how to ask the question without revealing that her lead had come from Ada Vail's private eye. Ada's refusal to cooperate with Curt had to have hampered the investigation. If she and Nick and Curt had worked together, perhaps the mystery would have been solved by now. Claire sipped at her coffee and decided that the way to pose the question would be to say she'd heard a rumor about Jonathan being in San Miguel but not to attribute the rumor to anyone. She heard a lot of rumors in her job; in fact, she was a lightning rod for Jonathan Vail rumors. Resolving that issue was easy, but posing her other question—whether Curt had really had breakfast in the Navajo Cafe the morning Tim died—appeared to be impossible. She didn't want to tip her hand. She also had no authority to question him. "What would you do, Nemesis?" she asked her cat, but he had no answer.

When she finished her coffee, Claire let the cat out and drove to work. There was no pressing business on her desk, so she began by calling Curt at his office. "How is the investigation going?" she asked.

"You'd have to ask Ellen Frank about Tim Sansevera. As for Jonathan Vail, nothing new. The duffel bag has not been found."

"The journal was authenticated by August Stevenson, a well-known handwriting expert."

"So Ellen said."

"I met with Lou Bastiann, the fan who is mentioned in the journal. He told me he sent Jonathan the briefcase from Saigon."

"Do you know how I can get in touch with him?" Curt asked.

"I don't, but Jennie does. I was going over some notes I have about Jonathan. Various people reported seeing him in the Mexican town of San Miguel de Allende. There was even a report that he was murdered there. I was wondering if you had ever heard any of those rumors, and whether you were able to substantiate or disprove them."

"Well," Curt paused and gave the query some thought. "I never heard that he was murdered in San Miguel de Allende, but I did hear that he was there. On the other hand, I also heard that he was in Denver, Santa Fe, LA, Seattle, and who knows where else? There were numerous sightings in the early years. I checked out the ones that were nearby, but I didn't have the resources to go far afield. I certainly couldn't go to Mexico. The fact that there were so many sightings seemed to take away the plausibility of any of them, but there's always the possibility that one or more were accurate."

"You never told me what you believe happened to him," Claire said.

"In all honesty, I don't know. The truth about the man was as elusive as a native trout. Luckily I only have eight months left to think about it."

Claire didn't believe he would stop thinking about it once he retired, but she didn't say so. She still wanted to ask him about breakfast in Bluff, but she couldn't think of a way to lead into it. Did he eat breakfast? What did he like for breakfast? Were there any restaurants in Bluff that he enjoyed? It seemed far too obvious to Claire, and her confidence in herself as an investigator was waning. "Thanks a lot for your help," she said. "If you ever get to Albuquerque, give me a call."

"I'll do that," Curt replied.

After she got off the phone, Claire considered how else she might find out whether Curt had told the truth about breakfast in Bluff. One way was to go there. It was a five-hour drive, but it wouldn't take very long to check out the Navajo Cafe. She didn't necessarily have to do it alone either.

She called the rancher, Sam Ogelthorpe, to ask if he would meet her. While the phone rang, she wondered if he'd be out on the ranch somewhere or if he had an answering machine.

She was somewhat surprised when he answered, "Howdy," on the fourth ring.

"Sam," she said. "This is Claire Reynier from the Center for Southwest Research."

"At the University of New Mexico?"

"That's right. I have to be in Utah this weekend, and I was wondering if you might be able to meet me in Bluff. My days are going to be pretty full, but I could meet you for breakfast."

"I get up early," Sam said.

"What time?"

"Five-thirty, but it'll take me a while to get over there. How about if I meet you at seven on Saturday?"

"It's a deal. How about the Navajo Cafe?"

"It's the only place I'd eat in Bluff."

"I'll see you there," Claire said. Her confidence had been restored to the point that she began making a list of the questions she had for Sam Ogelthorpe.

15

Chapter Fifteen

Before Claire left for Utah, she called John Harlan to see if he'd been able to locate the *Out of the Blue*'s.

"I found two of 'em," he said. "Neither was very valuable, and neither was written by Jennie Dell. Both have a man's photo on the dust jacket. One is a novel, one is the autobiography of a pilot."

"I'm on my way to Utah and could use some reading material for the trip. Could I stop by and pick them up?"

"Sure, but you'd have to be pretty desperate to want to read either of these books. A takeout menu would be more interesting."

"Let's say I'm more curious than desperate."

"On the subject of curiosity, are you going to tell me why you're going to Utah?"

"To talk to Sam Ogelthorpe again."

"Has that guy got anything to say that he hasn't already said a hundred times over?"

"He might, if I ask the right questions."

There was a pause before John said, "Could you use some company on your trip? I've been thinking about taking a weekend off."

"Thanks, John, but this is something I have to do by myself."

On her way to Page One, Too, Claire stopped and bought USGS topographic maps of Sin Nombre Canyon and the adjacent quadrants, including Comb Ranch. John was out when she got to his office, but he'd left the two *Out of the Blue*s on his desk, along with an invoice for thirty dollars and a note that read, "Call me on Monday. I'm expecting another *Out of the Blue*." Claire was incapable of picking up a book without checking its content and its condition. A brief glance at both books confirmed what John had already told her.

The traffic was heavy leaving town, and it took five and a half hours to get to Bluff, driving most of the way in darkness and missing the beauty of the red rocks east of Cuba. The fires at the oil refineries in Farmington blazed in the night. When Claire got to Bluff she found a motel and checked in at ten-thirty. Being a compulsive reader, she actually would have read the phone book or a takeout menu when she got into bed, if nothing else had been available. But she examined the books John left for her and found that he had been right. Jennie Dell wasn't the author of either of them, unless she'd been a ghost. The autobiography had an interesting subject, but the poor writing made it dull. The novel read as if it had been written by a graduate of the University of Iowa Writers' Workshop, which to Claire meant intensely personal observations ending in an epiphany that she couldn't share. She glanced at the author photo and bio on the back flap. The bio confirmed that the author had graduated from the University of Iowa. The photo showed him to be an earnest young man. The copyright page revealed that the book had been published in 1975. Twenty years had passed, and the Iowa style remained unchanged, a thought that Claire found depressing, since she believed that writing should reflect the times. She put the books down and by midnight was sound asleep.

She woke early and arrived at the Navajo Cafe at six-thirty, sitting at a table in the picture window and looking over the village of Bluff, which had a beautiful site, thick with cotton-woods, near the banks of the San Juan River. The town was a Mormon settlement that had been carved out of the wilderness at the cost of many lives, some of which were Mormon. A cemetery on top of the bluff commemorated their struggle.

Claire's waiter appeared wearing a T-shirt, a bandanna, and a name tag: Nelson. He had a round face and long black hair tied back in a ponytail. He was a big man, but soft-spoken, with a gentle, humorous manner. Claire thought he was most likely a Navajo, since the reservation was on the other side of the San Juan River. The waiters in Indian country had a way of lowering the volume and slowing the pace.

"High test or regular?" he asked.

"Regular," Claire laughed and told him she would wait till her companion arrived to order breakfast.

When Nelson returned with the coffee, she asked him if he knew Curt Devereux.

"Don't think so," Nelson said. "Does he live here?"

"He works for the Park Service."

"Those guys like to sit at Dolores's station. She's retired now, but her family's been havin' some health problems and she needs the extra cash, so she works here part-time. She still likes to keep in touch with what's happening. Want me to ask her to come over?" "Please," Claire said.

She watched Nelson cross the room and stop to talk to a waitress with ash blond hair pinned on top of her head with a clip. She wore jeans and hiking boots and had a muscular build and a no-nonsense manner. Dolores glanced briefly at Claire, then went back to serving her table. Claire sipped at her coffee and debated how to broach the subject of Curt Devereux. When Dolores had a free moment, she walked over, stood beside the table, and studied Claire with wary eyes that seemed to suggest she considered Claire too refined and too urban to trust. Since Claire was wearing a T-shirt and jeans herself, she wondered what signal she might have sent that she was a scholar or a nuisance.

"You want to talk to me?" Dolores asked.

"I'm looking for Curt Devereux. I heard he comes in here sometimes, and I was wondering if you knew how I could find him."

"He's working out of Gallup now. I don't see him much anymore. Last time he came in for breakfast was, oh, a couple of weeks ago."

"Do you remember what day?" Claire was pushing at the envelope of the circumspect limits she had set for herself and worried that she might be trying Dolores's patience as well.

"It had to be the last Saturday in October. That's when I started working the breakfast shift. If you really want to find him, you could check the ranger station. They'll know whether he's over this way or not."

"Thanks," Claire said.

"No problem." As Dolores walked back to her side of the cafe, Claire thought that although the alibi she'd given Curt wasn't airtight, it tended to substantiate his story. If Curt had been in the Navajo Cafe the morning Tim died, he couldn't have killed him. The owner of the white van parked at the entrance to Sin Nombre Canyon remained unaccounted for. Claire got out the USGS maps and was studying the terrain when Sam Ogelthorpe showed up, wearing his swooping black hat and dusty cowboy boots.

"You're here early." He sat down, took off his hat and laid it on an empty chair.

"I like the morning. It's the best time of day, don't you think?"

"Evening's not too bad."

Nelson arrived with two menus, and the conversation ceased while they ordered. Claire decided on bacon and hashbrowns. Sam had eggs over easy.

"What are you looking at?" he asked, eyeing the map.

"The way to get from Sin Nombre to your ranch."

"It's a direct route," he said. "You hardly even have to cross an arroyo." With the tines of his fork he traced the patch across Cedar Mesa. "Back when they used to let me graze my cattle in the canyons, I rode over there a lot. My tracks were clear in 1966. Jonathan followed my trail right up to my ranch. All he had to do after that was walk out to the road and hitch a ride to Mexico."

"Can you tell me what kind of a build the person you saw had?"

Sam shrugged. "Medium height. Slim-hipped."

"Would you say he was short-legged or barrel-chested?"

"No."

"What color was his hair?"

"Brown."

"Was it thick or frizzy?"

"No. It was long, but it wasn't frizzy." Sam's answers were quick and sure, considering the event had taken place more than thirty years ago, but it was also a story he had repeated often. Claire wondered how much it had lost or gained in the retelling.

"Did anyone fitting that description ever visit you?"

"Might have. A lot of people visited me back then. I may not remember all of them, but I do remember who I saw killing my cow."

"And you're positive it was Jonathan?"

"If it wasn't him, then it was a deserter, but what the hell would a deserter be doing in southeastern Utah? Where would he have deserted from?"

"What makes you think he was a deserter?"

"He was wearin' dog tags and a fatigue jacket."

"You didn't tell me that before."

"Didn't I? Well, I told Curt Devereux, and he made nothin' of it. Just some old hippie, he thought. It couldn't have been Jonathan 'cause he wasn't reported missing till two days later."

"Why are you so convinced he was headed for Mexico?"

"Where else would a deserter or a draft dodger go from here? It's a whole lot closer than Canada. With a little bit of money to pave the way, a guy could live out his life comfortably in Mexico. They've got no objection to criminals or draft dodgers as long as they've got the money."

Nelson brought breakfast, and that ended the conversation. Claire wondered whether Sam had any more information to give her, but as soon as breakfast was over, he remarked that much as he enjoyed visiting with her, he had to be on his way.

His departure left her wondering what to do with the rest of the day. It was still early. If she left now, she'd be home by early afternoon with no plans for the weekend. She considered stopping at the ranger station to see Ellen Frank, but how could she visit Ellen without admitting she'd been conducting her own investigation? Claire decided to drive back to Slickrock Canyon the long way through Blanding to avoid the tortuous climb up the Moki Dugway.

It took an hour to get to Mile Marker 23. When she stopped at the gate to let herself in, Claire noticed that fresh tire tracks in the dust had obliterated animal tracks left over from the night. She drove down the bumpy road to the fork. Today there was a Subaru station wagon parked under the cedars where the van had been. An SUV was parked in the right fork. A couple of backpackers were standing next to it, adjusting their loads and preparing to hike into the canyon.

Claire said hello, walked along the rim, and sat down at a place beside the stone cist where she could look out through an opening framed by a weathered gray beam. She never went hiking without her day pack containing trail mix and water, and now she took the pack off and drank from her water bottle. The cist could be a thousand years old, but, as far as she knew, it had never been established whether the structures on the canyon rims were used for storage or for lookouts. Food could be stored anywhere, but this was a spot from which the Anasazi could see their enemies approach. Lookout made more sense to Claire than storage. Glad to be alone in the silence of this place, she stared into the canyon, hoping to bring the mystery of the writer, the hero, and the student into focus.

A bird rode an updraft above the far rim. It had the white underbelly and wide wings of a red-tailed hawk. It tipped its wings as it circled, flapped once and flew away. Claire remembered seeing a redtail drop out of the sky and pick up a snake in its talons. She knew a hawk could spot a snake beneath a tree at a distance from which a human could see only the tree.

She imagined she was circling the sky herself, eliminating suspects, narrowing options, looking for a very particular prey, a prey who knew the duffel bag had reappeared in Sin Nombre Canyon and had a reason to covet its contents, a prey with access to a white van. There was one place left to look for the van, but Claire preferred to do it under cover of darkness, which gave her hours to fill. She passed the time by walking along the rim to the point where the sentinel rocks stood. She didn't see anyone else on her hike. She knew it was possible to spend days here without seeing another person. Remote and isolated as the canyons were now, they had been even more so in 1966. Whatever had happened here between Jonathan and Jennie was known only to them or to whoever else they had confided in.

Claire stayed on the rim thinking and observing, nibbling on her trail mix. When the shadows lengthened and the color of the sandstone deepened, she walked back to her truck. Both the vehicles she'd seen parked earlier were still in place, and there were no new hikers. Slickrock Canyon was hard to find. It took hours to hike in and out. The people who came here were likely to stay all day or camp deep in the canyon. The pattern was to arrive early and leave late. Yet when Ellen had flown over in the helicopter in mid-afternoon, the van was gone.

Claire left Slickrock, drove to Blanding, and had dinner at a restaurant decorated with wagon wheels. By the time she finished eating, it was dark. She drove back through Shiprock and Farmington, picking up a nearly full moon in Cuba that lit her way east. She reached I-25 at Bernalillo. This was where she ordinarily turned south to Albuquerque, but tonight she headed north. The clock on her dashboard read eleven-thirty. The timing was right, since she hoped to arrive at her destination near midnight. It had been a long day. She had accomplished a great deal and put several hundred miles on her car. She ought to be tired by now, but she wasn't. She should be nervous, but she didn't feel anxiety, either. All she felt was anticipation and a keen sense of awareness that brightened the moonlight and deepened the shadows.

When she reached the exit to Madrid, she turned south on Route 14, passing the New Mexico state pen, which was lit up like a landing pad. After the penitentiary, Claire didn't see another car. The road climbed into the Ortiz Mountains, shimmering like a river of silver. As she approached Madrid, the sculptures on the edge of town danced in the moonlight. The baseball diamond was ghostly white. The slag heaps were lumps of dark shadow. The town was fast asleep. The tourists were gone, and there were parking places for the taking.

Claire drove to the far side of town and parked beside a dirt road. She took a flashlight from her glove compartment, closed and locked her truck, and began walking toward Jennie Dell's, hoping all the dogs in town wouldn't hear her. Madrid was likely to be full of dogs, and it only took one sounding the alarm to set all of them howling. The brightness of the moon added substance to the shadows. The rustle of the wind gave them life. The backside of a cholla became a snakepit; a piñon, a bear; a low-lying juniper crept along like a coyote on the prowl. Potholes turned into sinkholes. Rocks became boulders. Claire was casting a long-legged shadow herself. She hoped no one was awake to notice and mistake her for a spirit or a thief.

The first few houses she passed were quiet and dark. When she reached the converted schoolhouse, she heard a dog give a low growl. She stopped and stood perfectly still, wishing she could call in her shadow and squash it beneath her feet. The combination of her shadow and her body made her far too long and visible. The dog stood on the embankment next to the schoolhouse, looking large and mean. She had come from the wilderness to a place where domesticated dogs ruled the night. Stay calm, Claire said to herself. The dog stared at her for a long minute, then yawned and lay down on the ground. Claire started walking again.

The dog barked and she turned to stone. She knew it was better not to turn her back on an alarmed dog, better to walk toward it with her arm extended, palm open in a gesture of offering and appeasement—an empty gesture at the moment, since she had nothing to offer. She wished she'd filled her pockets with kibble somewhere on her journey. Another option was to pick up a rock and pretend to throw it at the dog, an action that would intimidate a coward but aggravate a bully. Claire decided to try another quiet step forward. The dog barked again, sounding a warning to all its kin. A bark answered from the far side of town. Claire stopped. The dog stood still. It was possible that dogs in Madrid barked so often and so loud that no one even woke up, but she didn't want to risk it. She bent over, fluffed out her hair, unzipped her windbreaker and filled it with air. Then she leapt up, flapping the windbreaker, shaking her hair, hissing low in her throat, pretending to be a creature from another universe—a skinwalker, a demon, an alien. The dog stared, jumped back, then put its tail between its legs and ran away.

Claire continued down the road, turning wary as she approached Jennie Dell's house. If Jennie happened to look out the window, she would see Claire, but would she recognize her? The midnight prowl was so out of character, Claire wasn't sure she would recognize herself. She came around a bend in the road and stopped in front of Jennie's. The house that had appeared so bright and sunny during the day hid dark secrets at this time of night. Moonlight bleached the color out of the clapboards. The windows facing the street were blank.

Jennie's Honda was parked in the driveway, with a motorcycle parked right behind it. Claire walked up close and found what she'd expected to find—the bike had Missouri plates. She wondered whether the owner shared Jennie's bed as well as her driveway. She'd seen tension between them, but that didn't necessarily keep people from sharing a bond or a bed. Peering through the windows was dangerous, and she had come here on another mission to discover what was in the shed. The doors to the shed, wide enough to admit a vehicle, opened from the sides and joined in the middle. They were locked shut with a padlock. Claire walked up and shook the lock gently, but it held. She circled the shed, hoping to find another way to see inside. The wall away from the house had weathered siding, and so did the rear. Neither had a window or a door. After she'd examined the far side and the rear, Claire braced herself against the wall and peered cautiously around the corner of the wall that faced Jennie's house. The lip of a windowsill protruded from the far end of the wall near the shed door, but it faced a window in Jennie's house. Claire reviewed the layout of the house, trying to remember what room was on this side. The kitchen, she thought, which was unlikely to be in use at this time of night. She took a cautious step toward the shed window.

A spotlight mounted on the side of the house snapped on, activated by motion or a suspicious resident. The light widened and formed a pod where it landed on the ground beside the house. It didn't reach as far as Claire. In fact, it made the place where she stood darker in contrast, but if the light woke someone in the house and that person came outside or looked beyond the beam of the spotlight, Claire was clearly visible. She thought about running, but knew that movement made a prey easier to see. She pressed herself against the wall of the shed;

trying to be invisible. She wondered if she could have activated the motion detector from this distance, but then she saw what had set it off. Butterscotch stepped onto the front stoop, extended his front legs, stretched, and curled his tail.

If the light could be turned on this easily, Claire didn't think Jennie would pay much attention to it. Madrid was a place where pets became active at night. Still, Claire wanted the light off before she proceeded any further. The only way to do that was to put Butterscotch to sleep or lure him away from the stoop. Claire was relieved that the animal was a cat and not a dog, she knew cats better. She had a high-pitched whistle that she used to call Nemesis. To her it sounded more like an insect or a bird than a human. Now she whistled to Butterscotch, who sat down, licked his paws, and ignored the summons. Claire didn't dare use her speaking voice, which could be heard and recognized. She whistled again. The cat looked her way but didn't deign to get off the step. Claire knew cats well enough to understand that to allow her safety to depend on getting one to obey a command was suicidal. It would be wiser to entrust her life to a coyote.

She picked up a stone and tossed it into a clump of hollyhock leaves beside the shed. As she had hoped, the stone rustled the dry leaves and aroused the cat's curiosity and hunting instincts. It leapt off the stoop, out of the range of the motion detector, and the light went off. Claire closed her eyes for a minute to let them readjust to the moon's lesser light. When she opened them again, Butterscotch was sniffing at the hollyhocks. She slid along the side of the shed, bent over, and picked up the cat, fearing it might scratch or howl, but it snuggled and purred in her arms.

"Good boy," she whispered, transferring the cat to her left arm, so the right was free for the flashlight. She was beside the window now, and she quickly beamed the flashlight in. Light landed on a white wall, the side of a van. Claire guided it around the rear of the vehicle until it came to the license plate. NEW MEXICO, USA, the letters said. A hot-air balloon floated behind the numbers. Claire snapped the flashlight off and put the cat down. "Thanks, Butterscotch," she whispered.

She walked along the far side of the driveway, concealing herself as well as she could behind the Honda and the motorcycle. She believed that one of the people inside the house was the owner of the white van and that neither of them was a person she wanted to encounter unarmed at night. After she passed Jennie's house, Claire turned around to give it a last look.

The motorcycle and Honda were still in place in the driveway. The windows were dark, but suddenly a light in an upstairs room that might have been the bathroom came on, silhouetting the shape of a man. She recognized the combination of soft stomach and hard arms that was Lou Bastiann. He stood still for a minute, looking at himself in the mirror, perhaps, while his shadow seemed to reach across the yard to end at her feet. She knew the interior light would make the exterior appear so dark he wouldn't be able to see her, but then he turned the light off, which put darkness on his side and moonlight on hers.

Standing still turned her into a suspect. Running would make her easy prey. Claire sensed that her best option was to turn her back and slowly and deliberately walk away, hoping she wouldn't be recognized if she was noticed. Her feet crunched the stones in the road. She didn't hear anyone behind her, but she didn't know for sure whether she had been followed until she reached her truck and turned around. The road was empty. If Lou had seen her, he had done nothing about it. Claire got in her truck and drove home through El

Corazón del Ortiz Ranch, thinking about what she had discovered and the connection between Jennie and Lou. Either of them, or both of them, might have driven the van to Slickrock Canyon and gone looking for the duffel bag. Veterans Day was this week. Lou had said he would be at the memorial in Angel Fire and Jennie had confirmed it. Claire preferred to question him without Jennie around, and she hoped she could do it at the service. As for Jennie, Claire thought the truth about her was less likely to be found in conversation than between the pages of a book.

16

Chapter Sixteen

It was two o'clock in the morning when Claire got home. She picked up her cat, gave him a hug, and checked the messages. There was only one, and it was from John Harlan. "I found your book," he said. "It's the *Out of the Blue* that was published in 1963."

"Yeah!" Claire said to herself. She was too excited to go to sleep right away, so she took a hot bath scented with lavender oil. She lay in the tub and calculated how old Jennie Dell would have been in 1963. The fullness of her face, which tended to plump out fine lines, and the retro clothes and hairdo made her age hard to guesstimate. Jonathan was twenty-three when he disappeared in 1966. Claire figured Jennie's age to be within five years of Jonathan's. If she were five years younger, she would have been fifteen in 1963. Five years older would have made her twenty-five. Young to have published a novel, in any case. Sitting in the steaming water and doing mental arithmetic put Claire to sleep, which was where she wanted to be, but she would rather have awakened in a warm bed than a tub full of cold water. She dried herself off and went to bed, but had trouble falling asleep again. She was so close to solving the mystery that, unless the solution came to her in a dream state, time spent sleeping seemed a waste, yet she needed sleep so she would be alert when she read Jennie's book. She dropped off around four and woke up again at eight. For Claire, her fifties had become an adventure in sleeplessness. She knew exactly how many hours it took to get by. Eight was an unobtainable fantasy. She could function on six. Five was marginal. Four was pushing her limits. Less than that became dangerous. She hated to drive or think on less than four hours' sleep.

When she woke up, she looked out the window and saw that it was another beautiful fall day. She let Nemesis out, did her more militant tai chi exercises—felling the tree, repulsing the monkey, and embracing the tiger. Then she made a cup of coffee and called John Harlan. It was nine o'clock on Sunday morning, but he was already at the store.

"I've been wonderin' when you would call," he said.

"I got home at two this morning. I expected you to be asleep at that hour."

"What were you doing coming home at two in the morning?"

"It's a long story. Are you sure the book is Jennie's? As I recall, the *Out of the Blue* from 1963 was written by someone named Jess Moran." With that name Claire had no idea whether the author was male or female.

"The author's name is Jess Moran, but the photo on the back flap is of a young, blond hippie. It fits all the descriptions I've ever seen of Jennie Dell."

"Did you read it?"

"Yup. It's a coming-of-age novel set in southern California and Yosemite in the late fifties and early sixties."

"Was it any good?"

"Let's talk about it after you've had a chance to read it."

"How did you find it?"

"A dealer in California had a copy. I think the reason you and I never heard about it was that it was set mostly in Southern California. It was hard to consider Southern California as the Southwest even in 1963."

"Southern California is Southern California."

"Right," John agreed. "Shall I bring the book over?"

"I'll pick it up," Claire said, although she didn't feel like driving.

"I'll tell you what. Why don't we meet halfway, at Marie's for coffee?"

"It's a deal," Claire said.

Before she left, she dressed in jeans, combed her hair, and put on some makeup. There were dark half circles, the flip side of crescent moons, beneath her eyes. Her neck had a crepey texture, making her think the effort Jennie put into looking young could be worth it.

John was sitting at a table at Marie's when Claire arrived. He stood up, kissed her cheek, and handed her the *Out of the Blue* by Jess Moran, which Claire immediately opened to the author's picture on the back flap. It was Jennie. The young Jennie. A thin Jennie whose face was defined not by the fullness of time but by its bone structure and expression. Her eyes were bold, and her expression was daring. Jennie's thick blond hair was parted in the middle, the same way she wore it today. She had a choker around her neck and wore long beaded earrings.

"That's her?" John asked.

"It is." Claire had no doubt.

"She must have been writing under a pseudonym."

"Or living under one. For all we know, Jess Moran is the real name and Jennie Dell the pseudonym."

Continuing her examination of *Out of the Blue*, Claire checked the publisher's logo on the spine. It was a New York imprint that had long since been swallowed up, digested, and eliminated by the consolidation of a media empire. The copyright page said the book was published in 1963 and gave Jess Moran's birth date as 1943, which would make her the same age as Jonathan. It was obvious immediately to Claire that *Out of the Blue* was a book known in the business as a small book, not so much for its physical size as for the size of the print run. The fact that the author's name was below the title and both were in small letters, the subtle colors and indifferent artwork on the jacket, the lack of glitter and embossing all said this was a book with limited expectations and a small budget. In the nineties a book that a publisher had any intention of promoting weighed a couple of pounds and had silver or gold embossed letters on the jacket, and a red or black background. What would make a book stand out now, Claire thought, was quietness, smallness, subtlety. She didn't recall as much glitz in 1963, but even so, *Out of the Blue* was obviously a book the publisher hadn't spent any money on promoting, a book that had been left to sink or swim on its own.

Claire read the acknowledgments and the dedication. The book was dedicated to the author's mother, and she recognized none of the names in the acknowledgments. There was nothing left to do but to read it. She couldn't do that here in the restaurant in front of John Harlan, but she did skim the first paragraph. Claire could usually tell from the first paragraph whether or not an author could write. It was clear from the very first sentence that Jess Moran had style. It was a hook that pulled the reader in and made Claire forget just how tired she was. She wanted nothing more than to go home and finish *Out of the Blue*, but John Harlan was sitting across the table, laughing.

"Do you really want any coffee?" he asked.

"No," Claire admitted.

"Take the book home. Read it. Promise you'll call me when you're done."

"I promise," Claire said.

It was a promise she didn't keep immediately. When she got home she took the book to her courtyard, grateful for the pleasant weather and the sunny seclusion. Warm days in November reminded Claire of a visit to an aging parent; you never knew if each one would be the last. One day you would look up, and all the leaves would be gone from the trees. It would be winter. The parent would be dead. Not that winter in New Mexico was severe, but she was a desert rat and not used to the cold.

She sat down on the banco and read *Out of the Blue* straight through. It was a short book—a novella, actually—and she was a fast reader. While she read, the shadows moved over the courtyard walls. A datura pod burst and spilled its seeds on the bricks without her noticing. When she finished, she felt she was coming up for air after a deep immersion. She put the book down, too stunned to move or speak. All she could do was sit on the banco soaking up the sun like a pool of still water.

Out of the Blue was a lean book, a book in which silence and space were used nearly as effectively as words. The dialogue struck Claire as accurate, capturing both the emotion of the characters as and the period in which it was set. In a sense it was a coming-of-age novel, but mostly it was the story of a daughter's rebellion against an overbearing mother. It was a corrosive relationship. The story was set in the sixties, and the rebellion took the form of sex and drugs. As the daughter became wilder, the mother became more entrenched. The book ended with no resolution, but the sense that this battle would continue until both parties were in the grave. The portraits of the mother and the daughter were remarkable, the writing style terse and effective. The daughter liked to escape to Yosemite and the rougher shores of the California coast. The title came from the thoughts she had while watching the surf. Claire thought the nature passages were brilliant. Jess Moran had a strong sense of place and a flair for metaphor. In fact, at one point, while on an acid trip, she described a rock wall at Yosemite as slipping and sliding like the walls of La Sagrada Familia.

Why, Claire wondered, had she never heard of a novel as good as this one? It should have become a *Catcher in the Rye* or *A Blue-Eyed Boy*, not a book that John Harlan had to spend days tracking down. She suspected that *Out of the Blue* had sold a couple of thousand copies, mostly to libraries, and had never come out in paperback, where it would have received a wider audience. The copies that remained in the publisher's warehouse most likely became pulp. With a sales history like that, it would be hard for the author to sell another book.

Had *Out of the Blue* disappeared because the publisher abandoned it or because the subject was a mother/daughter relationship? Or was the fact that the subject was a mother/daughter relationship the reason the publisher abandoned the book? If publishers believed books about mothers and daughters wouldn't sell, the belief became a self-fulfilling prophecy. But times had changed. *Thelma and Louise* had popularized the chick-flick genre. Publishers knew now that women bought most of the books, and they geared their marketing efforts accordingly. Claire was hard-pressed to recall exactly when the change took place, but she knew it was after 1963. In 1963 male taste defined what got read.

Claire absorbed these thoughts until the sun had moved over to the West Mesa and the entire courtyard was in shadow. She realized it was dinnertime and remembered she had promised to call John Harlan. There were few objective standards for judging a work of fiction; reading it was a subjective experience. She wanted to know if John, whose taste she respected, agreed with her. It might be a good time to invite him to dinner, since the need to talk about *Out of the Blue* would overshadow any thoughts of romance.

Claire went to her kitchen to see if she had anything to offer him for dinner. As a single woman who watched her weight, most of the food she kept in the house had to be cooked. There were no snacks, no chips, no ice cream, no candy. The shelves of the refrigerator were empty ribs. The bagels and tortillas were frozen. The only food that could be eaten raw were the carrots and the pears in the vegetable bin. Claire poured herself a glass of Chardonnay and considered her options. She had frozen pasta and frozen chicken. John wasn't much of a gourmet pasta eater, so she decided to try the chicken.

He was still at the store when she called. "What did you think of the book?" he asked her.

"I thought it was wonderful," she admitted. "Beautifully written."

"Me, too," John agreed. "Whether she's telling the truth or not, our Jennie can write."

Someone could write, thought Claire. Although truth was important in life, it had little relevance in fiction. "It's hard to believe such a good book could just disappear."

"It happens all the time, books slipping into the river like fish that get away."

"That's depressing, especially when you consider all the terrible books that survive." It seemed as good a time as any to invite him. "Would you like to come over for dinner and talk about it some more?" Claire asked.

"When?"

"As soon as you're finished at the store."

"Give me half an hour," John said.

Claire turned on the oven and put the chicken in a pot with curry powder, onion, sliced yams, almonds, and raisins. She had a well-loved clay pot that could start the chicken frozen and keep it tender. She poured herself another glass of wine, lit a fire in the fireplace, and was straightening up the living room when John rang the doorbell. It was his first visit to her house.

"This is a nice place," he said.

"I like it," Claire replied.

"It looks like you."

"Oh?"

"It's calm and peaceful."

"And gray," Claire added.

"How about subdued?" John said.

Although Claire always felt subdued, she didn't feel very calm or peaceful at the moment. She poured John a glass of wine, and while they waited for the chicken to cook, they sat in the living room and resumed their book talk.

John leaned back into the sofa, sipped his wine, and asked, "Would you say *Out of the Blue* is as good as *A Blue-Eyed Boy*?"

"Almost," Claire replied.

"Did you see any similarity?"

"Both are about rebellion. In terms of style, both are rather spare, but the authors have a feeling for nature and a flair for metaphor." In fact, there was an instance where the authors had used the same metaphor, but John hadn't read the journal yet and Claire wasn't at liberty to show it to him, so she kept the reference to La Sagrada Familia to herself.

"But one was written by a man . . ." John began. "And the other by a woman." It rattled Claire that she was finishing John's sentences for him, so she went to the kitchen to check on the chicken.

When she came back she had the sense that their conversation was a ball of yarn John balanced between his fingers, waiting for her to pick up the thread. She didn't, so he did it for her. "An interesting puzzle, isn't it? Two books, similar stories, one written by a man and one by a woman. The one written by the man becomes a classic, the one written by the woman disappears. Why do you think?"

"Timing. Luck. The one written by the man got more promotion from the publisher. It stayed in print long enough to find its audience. The author was a prominent figure who vanished. *Out of the Blue* was a very personal book. The background of protest in *A Blue-Eyed Boy* may have given it a more universal appeal."

John watched her over the rim of his wineglass. "Just for the heck of it, let's suppose they were written by the same person. Would you say the author was a man or a woman?"

Claire phrased her answer carefully. "I think it would have been easier for a woman to write like a man in the early sixties than for a man to write like a woman. People with less power study the people with more power, and they understand them better. On the other hand, August Stevenson authenticated the journal by comparing it to the handwriting of Jonathan in the center's archives, including letters, a previous journal, and the manuscript of *A Blue-Eyed Boy*. There was a difference in style between the journal and *A Blue-Eyed Boy*, but the handwriting was definitely Jonathan's."

"*A Blue-Eyed Boy* was handwritten?"

"It was typed, but there were extensive handwritten corrections."

"Which could prove that Jonathan edited it, not necessarily that he wrote it."

"Maybe the novels were written jointly," Claire suggested, although she didn't believe it. "There are couples who are capable of writing books together."

"It might be possible for two people to know each other's thoughts so well that they write in the same style." John stared into the fire, and Claire knew he was remembering his deceased wife, with whom he'd had a deep and lasting rapport.

Since the idea of trying to write a book or even share a metaphor with her ex-husband, Evan, was enough to put out her own fire, Claire turned her thoughts to her investigation while John reminisced. For her, it had always been a given that Jonathan wrote *A Blue-Eyed Boy* and that, if he were still alive, he would have come back and claimed the attention and recognition due him. But if Jennie had written the book and Jonathan were still alive, it would be hard to predict the actions of both of them.

John shrugged off his melancholy and said, "You've noticed, of course, that both books used 'blue' in the title?"

"I wouldn't attach much significance to that. Amazon.com lists twelve hundred books with 'blue' in the title."

"Twelve hundred?"

"Twelve hundred." Claire checked her watch. "The chicken should be done." They got up, and she put another log on the fire to keep it going until dinner was over.

One thing Claire had always been able to count on in life was her clay pot. She thought the chicken came out well—tender, subtly spiced, delicious—but John appeared more interested in talking about Jonathan Vail than he was in eating.

"Did you learn anything new in Utah?" he asked, spearing a slice of yam and balancing it on the end of his fork.

"Sam Ogelthorpe told me the man he saw in his ranch in 1966 wore dog tags and an army fatigue jacket. He said if the man wasn't Jonathan, he believed he was a deserter."

"I'd never heard that one before."

"Neither had I, but Sam claims he told Curt Devereux. Ada Vail wouldn't allow me to show you the journal, but I think it would be all right to tell you that it mentions a fan named Lou Bastiann. I met him, and he claims he was in Vietnam in 1966. The journal never says that Lou was in Slickrock Canyon and Jennie denies it, yet Tim Sansevera claimed he saw a duffel bag in the cave when he found the journal. When Curt and I went back to the cave, the duffel bag was missing, and it still hasn't been found. There's always the possibility that the duffel bag was Lou's, and that he went back to claim it."

"Why would he do that?"

"It explains what happened to Jonathan."

"Does he look enough like Jonathan that Sam could have confused them?"

"He doesn't now; he's got gray hair and he's heavier than Jonathan was. He might have looked very much like him in 1966, though. He has brown eyes, but Sam was too far away to see the color."

"There must be a way you could find out if a person was in Vietnam and when." John still hadn't put the yam in his mouth and it quivered on the end of his fork. "Have you searched the Internet?"

"No," Claire said, and she didn't intend to. She believed the information she wanted could be found at the Vietnam Veterans Memorial in Angel Fire. She'd made up her mind to go there for the ceremonies on Tuesday and confront whatever she found then.

John put the yam down and put a piece of chicken in his mouth. While he chewed, he pushed the rest of his meal around his plate, separating the raisins, almonds, and yams from the chicken and onions. A picky eater, Claire thought, a meat-and-onions man. The chicken and onions would be gone when the meal was over, but the yams, raisins, and almonds would still be on his plate. She hadn't given him the datura test, but he was failing the dinner test miserably and the confidence test as well. This was her opportunity to tell him the rest of the story—the visit to Otto, the van in Jennie's garage—but she didn't do it. There were many ways a man and a woman could be compatible and incompatible. It was possible to enjoy talking to someone and not enjoy having sex with him. She'd never actually had the experience, but she was sure the reverse was true. Eating dinner with a man ought to be a prelude. If he didn't like your cooking at its best, how would he feel about your less-than-perfect body?

She hadn't lit the candles, and the overhead light was harsh, laying shadows beneath their plates and turning John's uneaten yams a garish orange. The wine was wearing off, and Claire felt the ragged edge of sleeplessness. It was either have another glass of wine to revive herself or show John the door when dinner was over.

Claire cleaned her plate. John finished the chicken and the onions, and put down his knife and fork. He peered down the hallway toward the living room, anticipating, perhaps, the sofa, the fire, a renewal of the previous conversation or the beginning of a different dialogue.

"I appreciate all the help you've given me, John," Claire said. "But I didn't get any sleep last night and I'm very tired. I need to go to bed."

"Can I help you clean up?"

"There's nothing to it. All I have to do is put the uneaten food in the refrigerator and the dishes in the dishwasher."

"Thanks for the dinner. I enjoyed it very much."

"You did?"

"Yes," John said. "Let's do it again." Claire walked him to the door. On her way back through the living room she shut the glass door to the fireplace and closed the vents, depriving the fire of oxygen and letting it go out.

17

Chapter Seventeen

Veterans Day was celebrated in the eleventh month on the eleventh hour of the eleventh day. Claire had 165 miles to drive to get to the memorial at Angel Fire. She needed to leave by seven to be sure she'd make it by eleven. She explained her absence from the library by implying she'd be looking at a rare book collection in Taos, 35 miles from Angel Fire. Before she went to bed Monday night, she looked out her window at the sky. The nights in New Mexico were usually so clear that she could follow the moon in all its phases, but tonight clouds sat on top of the Sandias. The forecast predicted blustery winds and a temperature that would dip into the low twenties.

When Claire woke in the morning the clouds had lifted, turning into gray wings hovering over the peaks like sinuous falcons. The mountains had received a dusting of snow, and the wind had blown the remaining leaves off the trees. The winter she had been anticipating had arrived. The normally muted desert colors of blue and brown had been replaced by Arctic white and brooding gray. If there was snow on the Sandias, there was likely to be more snow farther north. Driving in snow made Claire uneasy, but she was determined to get to Angel Fire.

The interstate was clear to Santa Fe, and there was little traffic this early in the day. The Sangre de Cristos wore a white blanket, but the city hadn't gotten any snow, making Claire optimistic that she wouldn't see any more until she approached the higher elevations near Taos. North of Santa Fe she saw three gray falcon clouds hanging together in the east. She lost sight of them when she dipped down near the river north of Española on Route 68, which snaked along the Rio Grande through a deep and rocky ravine. The road was dry here, and the ribbon of sky that Claire could see was robin's egg blue. She looked at her clock and saw that she was making good time. At this rate she would get to Angel Fire early, which would give her a chance to do some investigating before the ceremony began. The memorial was full of resource materials—books, computers, photographs, handwritten notes.

The highway passed through the villages of Velarde, Embudo, and Pilar and then it began to climb, winding up out of the ravine onto a vast plateau that offered one of the most spectacular views in New Mexico. Claire always felt that she was coming from a dream state into full consciousness here, out of the underworld and into the light. Today the mesa was spread with a white cloth. The mountains were a slate colored backdrop. The gray clouds that Claire had seen earlier had reappeared, but had shifted so they were stacked on top of each other like a flotilla of flying saucers. There had been snow on the road, but most of it had run off or melted.

Right before Taos, Claire turned east on Route 64, which gained elevation as it passed through the ponderosa pines of Carson National Forest. The snow was deeper here, covering the ground and weighing down the pine branches. There were places where the trees shaded the road and the snow lingered in the shadows. Claire drove carefully, gripping the steering wheel, fearing that she would come around a curve, hit a snowy patch, and spin out.

It was a relief to leave the woods and enter the wide-open Moreno Valley, the largest valley Claire had seen anywhere. Here the sun had warmed the road and melted the snow. The valley was a field of white. Eagle Nest Lake danced in the wind. The runway of the Angel Fire airport pointed at the cloud formation Claire had been watching, which had realigned so it graduated in size from top to bottom, giving the effect of perspective. The air was so clean that Claire felt she could taste the freshness. It was a day that had wings, a good day and a good place to go looking for the truth.

The Vietnam Veterans Chapel sat on a hill looking across the Moreno Valley. Claire saw its sweeping lines as the prow of a ship or swept-back wings, although she knew that from the back side it could be seen as arms open in a welcoming gesture. The white stucco exterior had the rough texture of ruffled water. Dr. Victor Westphall, who had built the chapel as a memorial to his son David, believed the area was sacred ground, that a line of force emanating from Wheeler Peak, the highest point in New Mexico, passed right through the site of the memorial.

As Claire drove up the hill to the parking lot, she checked the clock on her dashboard again. It was ten-fifteen, and the lot was filling with vehicles. Many were junkers, older beat-up models of trucks or subcompacts. The sun broke through the clouds and shone on the lot, highlighting the shabbiness of the vehicles. Claire read the bumper stickers as she circled the lot: NEVER FORGET THE VIETNAM VET, UNIVERSITY OF SOUTH VIETNAM, SUPPORT YOUR POW/MIA's. Although the majority of license plates were from New Mexico, many other states were represented. Claire didn't see any vehicles she recognized, and she wondered whether anyone would recognize her. Her truck was anonymous enough in some ways. It had no bumper stickers, distinguishing dents, or dings, but it did have a UNM parking sticker on the windshield. She hoped her presence would be unexpected, and no one would think to look for her truck or to check her windshield.

She parked at the far end of the lot, locked her cell phone and camera in the truck, and walked downhill to the memorial. In addition to the chapel, there was a visitors center with a library, an auditorium, and an exhibition area. A triad of flagpoles stood at attention in front of the visitors center. The flags of New Mexico, the United States, and POW/MIA snapped in the wind. The people who milled around in front of the building wore denim and fringe, looking like faded hippies and ragtag warriors.

Claire walked back up the path and entered the chapel, which was always left open so people could visit at any time of night or day. The contrast between the narrow, dank interior of the chapel and the vast, white Moreno Valley was striking. Inside was an altar with a slit for a window. Offerings were placed in front of a wreath full of miniature flags. Vietnam-era music played in a constantly revolving tape, and Jane Fonda was always out of favor. David Westphall had lost his life in an ambush during the Tet Offensive in 1968. The loss of the son became an obsession of the father. Sometimes Claire thought he should have accepted the loss and let go of it a long time ago, but she knew that his obsession had brought comfort to many. The chapel saddened her, and she didn't linger.

She went outside and walked back up the path, checking the parking lot again on her way to her truck. By now the lot was full. A white Dodge van with New Mexico balloon plates had taken a space at the end of the lot nearest the highway. Claire walked past the van, noted that it seemed unoccupied, and continued on to her pickup. She unlocked the door, took out her camera, inserted her telephoto lens, and looked through it, pretending to be photographing the view, but in reality checking to see if anyone was watching. She didn't see anyone she recognized or anyone who showed her undue attention, so she went back to the van. The rear window was covered with calico curtains and so was the one on the side, but the side curtains didn't quite meet. Claire walked to the front of the van, looked through the windshield, and made sure no one was inside. The front seats hid much of the interior, but through the space between the seats she could see the handlebars of a motorcycle, a motorcycle she was sure had Missouri plates. It was close to the eleventh hour, and the service was about to begin. Claire saw a couple of people heading away from her down the path, but no one else remained in the parking lot. She tried the handle of the side door and wasn't surprised to find it locked tight. She put her forehead against the glass and peered into the space between the curtains, grateful for the New Mexico sun that blasted through windshields, and X-rayed parked vehicles, turning them into ovens. The window let in just enough light so she could see the olive drab duffel bag that lay on the floor beside the motorcycle. A serial number and the name Louis Bastiann were written on the bag in large black letters. Claire had no doubt that this was the bag that had been in the cave in Sin Nombre Canyon and that, if she examined it, she would find a layer of Utah dust. Unless she broke a window, though, she could only guess what the bag contained. Breaking and entering went beyond the scope of the investigating Claire would allow herself. She walked behind the van and memorized the license plate number, then turned and went to the visitors center.

The service had begun. Claire looked through the door of the auditorium and saw that every seat was taken. People leaned against the walls with their backs to enlarged photographs of soldiers and Vietnamese children. The lectern was draped with an American flag. She had picked up a program in the foyer, and she used it to identify the people sitting on the dais: Dr. Westphall, who was in his eighties now; a woman poet; a male folksinger; an elder from the Taos Pueblo; a chaplain and an army colonel wearing a well-decorated uniform. The only faces Claire could see were those of the people who sat on the dais or leaned against the wall. Mostly she was looking at the backs of heads, which was enough to tell her that the audience was a New Mexican mix of Anglo, Indian, and Hispanic, about 60 percent male, largely middle-aged. She saw gray heads, blond heads, bald heads, heads of shiny black hair. The chaplain stood up and opened the service with a prayer.

Claire left the auditorium and went to the library, grateful for the chance to have it all to herself. She ignored the computerized educational display and looked at the bulletin board, which had a supply of blue Post-its for leaving messages. There were dozens of them stuck to the board, with the ends curling out. Vets sharing their struggles, their memories, their dreams, their poems. Vets looking for other vets. Children of vets searching for information about fathers who had died in combat. One young woman left a memorial for her grandfather, the drawing of a tombstone inscribed RIP, a poignant reminder to Claire that those who served were her age or older and could well have grandchildren by now. Veterans Day eventually became a ceremony for old men, men who had lost their fire, but she didn't see that happening yet. She read through the messages, wondering if there might be one that had meaning for her, half listening to the service in the auditorium. The chaplain finished his prayer, the poet read a poem about a heart full of fire, and Claire found a thought in a handwriting that she found familiar. "Sometimes life is a flowing river, sometimes it's a well run dry. A name or legend carved in stone lives forever." The unsigned message wasn't carved in stone. It had been written with a ball-point pen on a blue Post-it attached to the bulletin board by a sticky substance that enabled Claire to remove it and put it in her pocket.

The colonel began to speak. His voice was amplified by a microphone, and Claire could hear him clearly when her attention wasn't focused on her search. He said that he had been a helicopter pilot in country whose job was to ferry out the wounded and the dead. "I came home with a concrete heart," he said, "that it took a chisel to break up." He talked about a ceremony he had attended at the Wall. It seemed inevitable, at a Vietnam event, that sooner or later someone would start talking about the Wall. Claire had been there and thought it was a magnificent tribute, reminding her in some ways of Victor Westphall's chapel—wings or arms emanating from a vanishing point. An end, but also a beginning. The colonel recounted the experience of touching a name he recognized and seeing his own reflection in the polished, black surface transforming into an image of the person he knew. Claire had had a similar experience. The colonel said there were a hundred thousand people at that ceremony and he could feel the eyes of one of them staring at him so intensely it made the hair stand up on the back of his neck.

On the table near the bulletin board Claire found the book that listed all the names inscribed on the Wall in alphabetical order. She opened it and began turning the pages, stopping for a minute to listen to the conclusion of the colonel's story. At the end of the ceremony, a man he didn't recognize came up and asked if he'd worn a helmet with a lightning bolt painted on the side. "Yes," the colonel replied.

"You flew me out in your chopper. You saved my life," the man told him.

Claire had come to the *B*'s in the book. She scrolled down until she found the name she'd been looking for, Louis Bastiann. There were more than 58,000 names, and duplication was to be expected, but there was only one Louis Bastiann. He died a month before Jonathan Vail disappeared. Time enough for the effects and duffel bag of the fan with no family to be shipped home to his hero. If Jonathan had been contemplating honoring his draft notice, the death of Lou, his fan and alter ego, could have been the straw that convinced him to flee. He'd been presented with a ready-made identity, the clothes and the dog tags, and an excuse—death might well be waiting for him in Vietnam, too. He had Jennie, who was willing to con law enforcement and give him two days' head start. He didn't even need to go to Mexico or Canada. He could travel most of the world as Lou Bastiann and never be discovered, planning, perhaps, that one day, if amnesty were ever granted, he would come back and finish out his life as Jonathan Vail. When Jonathan split, he was a little-known regional writer, but during the time he was gone, the mystery of his disappearance and the impact of *A Blue-Eyed Boy* turned him into a legend, a legend that Claire herself had hoped to perpetuate. If he'd come back as Jonathan Vail after amnesty was granted, would Jennie have been willing to let him go on being the hero and taking credit for a book she had written? What would his life have been like? Claire wondered. He would have faced the contempt of some for dodging the draft and of others for allowing his name to be put on a book written by someone else. He might have been full of doubt about his writing talent, troubled by the relationship with his family and with Jennie. If he reappeared as himself it would be as a flawed human being, but if he went on living as Lou Bastiann the legend of Jonathan Vail would survive. He could be both a legend and a man. "Sometimes life is a flowing river, sometimes it's a well run dry. A name or legend carved in stone lives forever."

But the discovery of the journal had changed everything, raising the issue of publication and giving Jonathan back some control of his destiny. Claire wondered who went to the cave to retrieve the duffel bag, Jonathan or Jennie or both? The van could belong to either of them. Jonathan could have used her address to register the vehicle in New Mexico even if he didn't actually live in the state or in the country. What had he or she been after? The duffel bag with the name Lou Bastiann on it could be seen as evidence that Lou had died and that someone was impersonating him. And there may have been something in the bag that one or both of them wanted. Tim might have come upon the person in the cave and stumbled into his own death. If that was the case, the evidence necessary to prove it was in the white van in the parking lot. Claire looked down at her hand, which was stalled beside the name of Lou Bastiann. There were close to 60,000 names in this book, men, mostly, Jonathan Vail's age—many more identities he could assume if he escaped from Angel Fire.

Claire had been so engrossed in her thoughts that she had stopped listening to the colonel's speech. It came as a surprise to hear the mixture of applause and ululation that followed. She closed the book, walked to the auditorium, and looked in. The audience was giving the colonel a standing ovation. Visibly moved by his speech, men and women hugged and cried. The folksinger asked for his guitar. The audience began to sit down. Claire didn't find Jennie Dell's blond head in the crowd, but the profile of Lou Bastiann/Jonathan Vail stood out. He wore a denim jacket and a bandanna folded into a headband. When she spotted him, she stepped out of the doorway. The folksinger began to sing "This Land Is Your Land," inviting the audience to join in.

18

Chapter Eighteen

Claire walked across the foyer and stepped outside into a day that had turned blustery. The trio of flags resembled dragons that coiled and snapped in the wind. The sinuous lenticulars she'd seen earlier had become billowing storm clouds. The air had the feeling of incoming snow. She looked over the Moreno Valley, considering her options, wondering whether Jonathan had seen her. If she had to confront him, she would prefer to do it when there were other people close by. The program listed several more speeches, indicating that the ceremony would continue for some time.

Her cell phone was in her car. She could use it to call Ellen Frank, but before she did, she stopped to consider the consequences of making the call. Her job had been to preserve the legend of Jonathan Vail, and the legend would be better served if she kept what she'd discovered to herself, which might also be what Harrison would prefer. Would he or Ada really want to learn that the prized archive was the work of a fraud? That Jennie Dell had been the author of *A Blue-Eyed Boy*? That Jonathan Vail had spent a good part of his life hiding out as Lou Bastiann?

While Claire considered her options and weighed her obligations, she hugged her arms to her chest to keep out the wind. It was too cold to stand outside and wait for long. She looked through the door to the visitors center and saw that the foyer had remained empty. There was no indication that Jonathan had seen her or had left the auditorium. Overriding any other consideration in her mind was the loss of Tim Sansevera's life. She began walking up the path toward her truck, eager to get out of the cold but feeling that her shoes were weighted with lead. The wind whirled, picking up dust and debris. The arms of the chapel reached out. Behind her the flags fluttered and flapped. Claire pulled up her collar to ward off the cold and kept her head down to keep the stinging dust out of her eyes.

She didn't hear footsteps, didn't know Jonathan was behind her until he tapped her shoulder. She spun around and faced him, knowing she was the one who had been deceived yet feeling she had just been found out. Jonathan wore dark glasses. The wind tugged the gray hair from his headband and curled it over his head.

"Claire?" he asked. "What on earth are you doing here?"

"Hello, Jonathan," Claire replied.

At first he seemed incredulous, tipping his head and staring at her through the dark lenses. "You know?"

"Yes."

He exhaled then, and his body language expressed relief, as if he'd just dropped a backpack that had long been a burden.

"We need to talk. Let's get out of the wind."

Claire felt no need to talk, but Jonathan took her elbow and edged her toward the chapel, pushing open the door that was never locked and guiding her inside. The chapel offered shelter, but the wind whistled around the prow and entered the building through crevices and cracks. The sixties tape played on, with music drifting in and out of audibility as if it were being transported from a distant concert on the wings of the wind. Claire heard Credence Clearwater Revival sing, "Have you ever seen the rain?" before the music faded out. There was a dampness inside the chapel that suggested the concrete walls hadn't set. She leaned against the stucco in the entryway, feeling faint and dizzy.

Jonathan leaned against the opposite wall and raised the dark glasses. He wasn't wearing the tinted lenses that had been his cover, and Claire saw the blue eyes that the writer had been famous for, the eyes of a young man buried in the wrinkles of middle age. Coyote eyes, she thought. Trickster eyes.

"How did you find out?" he asked.

"Lou Bastiann's name is on the Wall and listed in the book in the visitors center. He died in 1966."

"You must have had some reason for looking there," Jonathan insisted.

"I always believed that if Jonathan Vail were alive he would have come back and claimed the admiration due him. Then I tracked down Jennie's novel and read it. The similarities between her book and *A Blue-Eyed Boy* are obvious. If she wrote *Blue-Eyed Boy*, Jonathan Vail could be anywhere. He might have been the man Sam Ogelthorpe saw kill his cow or it might have been Lou Bastiann. I had only your word and Jennie's that Lou Bastiann was in Vietnam in 1966. I needed to find out for myself."

"Jennie's a better writer, but after *Out of the Blue* didn't sell, she couldn't find a publisher for her next book. I had a reputation, so she borrowed my name and my life for *A Blue-Eyed Boy*. She never should have told you she'd written a novel."

Probably not, Claire thought, but ego will out. "It's not human nature to publish a book and tell no one about it."

"Is it human nature to want to be a legend even if you know you don't deserve it?"

"That's difficult to say," Claire replied. "Few people ever have the opportunity."

The eyes that remained restless no matter what color they were settled briefly on Claire before darting away. "My life was either shaped by events I couldn't control or by opportunity. Take your pick. When the army sent me Lou's stuff after he died, it gave me a ready-made identity. I wasn't doing a very good job of being Jonathan Vail. Taking too many drugs. Not happy with my writing. My family was on my case. The relationship with Jennie was trouble. I knew I didn't want to go to Vietnam.

"I carried Lou's duffel bag into the canyons and hid it in the cave in Sin Nombre, along with my journal. I held a little ceremony in the cave, dropped some acid, turned myself into Lou. The writer became the fan. I caused a rock slide, thinking my identity and thoughts would stay buried until I was ready to dig them up. I never told Jennie about the duffel bag. She knew I was going to Mexico, but I didn't tell her for years that I had assumed Lou's name. No one could make her reveal it if she didn't know it.

"Time passed. I liked my expatriate life in San Miguel de Allende. When I told you Lou couldn't write anymore, that was the truth. I stopped writing and made a living repairing cars. After I injured my leg, I couldn't do that kind of work anymore, so I began crafting folk art sculptures out of spare parts. I have a reputation as a metal sculptor in Mexico.

"When I left the States I was known only as a regional writer. Who would have dreamed that while I was gone *A Blue-Eyed Boy* would become a bestseller and Jonathan Vail would turn into a legend? Jennie wouldn't have let me go on being the hero if I'd come back, so when amnesty was granted I stayed where I was. I return every year to renew my vehicle registrations. I visit Jennie, see how the legend is doing, come to Angel Fire to pay my respects to Lou. I avoid my family. I had my life. Jennie collected the royalties. It was an arrangement that worked for both of us until your graduate student found Jonathan's journal."

He stopped talking, and Claire began listening for some sign that the ceremony had ended—people talking outside, footsteps on the path, some indication that she and Jonathan weren't alone in the dank chapel—but all she heard was wind and Janis Joplin cackling as the tape continued to spin.

"I can explain about your student." Jonathan placed the palm of his hand against the wall near Claire's head and leaned close. She felt he had invaded her space, but she feared that stepping away might anger him. The headband and the vivid blue eyes were making him appear wilder and more dangerous.

"There's no need to explain anything to me," she said, pressing against the wall. She knew that while confession might be good for the confessor, it could be dangerous for the one who hears it. The duffel bag in the van was evidence. There were hundreds of miles between here and Mexico. Lots of time for federal investigators to find Jonathan if he drove away. At this point she would be more than happy to turn the investigation over to them.

"You're my archivist. You want to know all about me, don't

you?" he asked in a voice that had the pleading tone of a person who has kept his secrets for too long.

"I'm the keeper of the legend, not the keeper of the truth. If you have a confession to make, you should make it to the rangers."

Jonathan acted as if he hadn't heard her. His eyes went to the light beaming through the slit behind the altar. "It wasn't Jonathan's fault," he began. "Like being given Lou's identity in the first place. It just happened."

Given his identity change, it wasn't surprising that he would talk about himself in the third person, but Claire found the dissociation disturbing. The chapel began to feel claustrophobic. She wanted to be in her truck, cradling her cell phone in her hand, but she felt pinned in place by the strength of his arms.

"Jonathan was—still is—a person that things happen to. He hiked across the mesa to Sin Nombre. It took him a while to find it after all those years. He spent the night in the cave and in the morning was looking through the duffel bag, remembering, wondering if he should have gone to Vietnam, the defining event of his time, wondering if he had wasted his life. If he'd had the courage to look death in the face then it might have changed him for the worse or it might have changed him for the better. A young man came through the dust looking a lot like Jonathan did in '66. He had the ponytail, the anger, the confidence. He claimed the bag belonged to him, and he tried to grab it. The men fought. The student stumbled and fell off the cliff. Jonathan walked out across the mesa with the bag. He put it in a locker keeping it hidden from Jennie until he came up here.

"Jennie never knew—still doesn't know—that there was a duffel bag."

"The autopsy showed no sign that anyone had injured Tim," Claire said in a voice that tried to be soothing. "You should tell the Park Service what happened. Ellen Frank will listen."

"But will she believe?" Jonathan asked.

"If the evidence supports what you say."

"If she doesn't believe me it would mean the end of my freedom, the end of my creative life. The death of a legend."

"What is it you want from me?" Claire asked. "Forgiveness?"

"Silence. I want you to promise silence."

It would only take one day's silence, Claire knew, to get him back to Mexico where the chances of extraditing him were remote.

He moved in close and she smelled fear. Coming from him? From her? From both? They each had reason to fear the other. He could harm her or kill her. She could expose him and cause his imprisonment.

"Your job depends on preserving the legend, doesn't it?" he asked.

It didn't. Claire knew there were other jobs for her at the center if the legend of Jonathan Vail crumbled. The music played on while she worried that her thoughts were written on her face. She was unpracticed at the art of deception and incapable of letting him escape for even one day. Suppose he came to believe that the only way to silence her was to kill her? If he attacked before the ceremony ended, he could easily get away with it. There was a long moment, one more opportunity for Jonathan Vail to discover what he was capable of while Claire considered what she was capable of. Tai chi advised to yield when the opponent mounted an aggressive attack, but it was hard to yield with her back against the wall. There was the small animal defense of dropping to the ground and curling into a tight little ball. But Claire felt that was too weak to be effective. To fight back would arouse and provoke an attacker who happened to be strong enough to overpower her. Her one option was to stand tall, be still, be firm, do nothing to cause alarm.

"I . . . you . . . he," Jonathan hesitated. Both of his hands were against the wall now, on either side of Claire's head. He leaned over her, and she felt she was about to be crushed by a predator's dark wings.

"Don't, Jonathan," she cried.

The door swung open, light entered the chapel, and voices spoke.

"What did you think of the ceremony?" a woman asked.

"I liked it," a man replied.

Jonathan dropped his hands and stepped back. He turned, flipped up the collar of his jacket, said, "The legend is in your hands now," and walked out the door.

Claire slid down the wall until she was sitting on the floor.

"Are you all right?" the woman asked.

"I think so."

"Can I get you a glass of water or something?"

"I just need to sit still for a moment," Claire said.

When she felt she could negotiate again, she walked uphill to the parking lot. From here she could see most of the Moreno Valley: the lake, the highway, the slate-colored mountains, the stormy clouds, the wispy clouds. She watched the white van head downhill, wondering whether it would turn left or right when it reached the highway. Either route would get it to Mexico eventually. Jonathan turned right on Route 38. For several minutes the van was the only vehicle on the highway. Claire watched it head toward Angel Fire and become no larger than a snowflake, then she unlocked her truck, picked up her cell phone, dialed information, and asked for the number of the ranger station at Grand Gulch. It was a federal holiday, but she hoped Ellen Frank would be at work. When she came to the phone, it was a relief to hear her calm voice.

"I found the white van," Claire said.

"Where?"

"At the Vietnam Memorial in Angel Fire."

"Are you sure it's the right van?" It was Ellen's duty to be skeptical.

"There's a duffel bag inside imprinted with the name and serial number of Lou Bastiann."

"The guy mentioned in the journal?"

"Right."

"Is he driving the van?"

"No. It's on record at the memorial that Lou Bastiann was killed in Vietnam in 1966. Jonathan Vail is driving the van."

"Our blue-eyed boy?"

"Yes. He's been disguising himself as Lou Bastiann all these years."

"Why?"

"It's a long story, but it has to do with perpetuating his legend. He confessed to me that when he went back to Sin Nombre to get the duffel bag, he ran into Tim Sansevera. They struggled, he said, and Tim fell off the cliff."

"Did you get the license number of the van?"

"Yes." Claire gave her the number. "I believe he is on his way to Mexico."

"I'll get the state police on it. Are we going to find anything incriminating if we catch him? Any proof that that's the bag that was in the cave?"

"I hope so," Claire said. "If nothing else, it will be layered with Utah dust."

"Are you in any danger there?"

"No." Now that the ceremony was over, the parking lot was filling with veterans.

Jonathan made it all the way to Carrizozo before he was caught, still driving the van, still carrying the duffel bag. Ellen Frank called in the FBI. Forensics found specks of Tim's blood and a set of his fingerprints on a shirt in the van. Jonathan claimed that Tim's death was accidental, but he was charged with murder and held over until trial as a flight risk. The original manuscript of *A Blue-Eyed Boy* with Jennie's handwritten notes was also in the duffel bag. Jonathan admitted that he hid it there, without telling her, before he sealed the cave and escaped from Sin Nombre Canyon.

After he was arrested, Jennie claimed authorship of *A Blue-Eyed Boy*, making it possible for her to give up writing the mini books and get a contract for a novel.

As soon as the truth came out about Jonathan and *A Blue-Eyed Boy*, questions were raised as to whether he deserved an archive or an archivist, and Harrison was the first person to raise them. He set up a meeting with Claire and Ada Vail in his office. At the appointed hour he sat at his desk and Ada sat in her chair across from him. Neither of them stood when Claire entered the room.

Claire entered the room.

"Be seated, please," Harrison said, waving his hand to indicate the chair next to Ada.

Claire sat down, and Ada turned to say hello. Perhaps it was the overhead light in Harrison's office, but she seemed older. A few strands of hair had pulled loose from the bun and framed her face. Her skin had the texture of a dry riverbed. Her lipstick bled into the cracks around her mouth. She wore a severe black dress. "Good to see you," she said in a voice that belied the sentiment.

"You, too," Claire replied. "Have you visited Jonathan?"

"In prison?" Ada asked.

In prison, thought Claire. He is your son. She didn't expect her own son ever to turn up in prison, but she knew that if he did she would be there.

"For more than thirty years Jonathan hid out, dodging the draft, masquerading as someone else, letting me believe he was dead, breaking his father's heart. I have nothing to say to him."

"You might find something, if you went to see him," Claire replied. "Did you know, for example, that he is a sculptor in Mexico?"

"No," Ada replied.

"It would have been better for the center if none of this had come out," Harrison said, forming a tent with his long white fingers and aiming the tip of it at Claire.

"There are other issues than what's good for the center, Harrison," Claire replied. "The death of Tim Sansevera, for one."

"That was unfortunate, to be sure," Harrison said, although his tone of voice implied he considered it a nuisance more than a tragedy. "The committee and I don't see the need for maintaining a Jonathan Vail archive any longer. We consider it an unnecessary expenditure of time, energy, and money on a man who has been proven to be a fraud."

It was pretty much what Claire had expected. Nevertheless, she replied, "Jonathan wouldn't be the first fraud to be honored by historians. His papers may no longer have value as a contribution to the literature of the Southwest, but they do have historical interest."

"I do not wish to see my son honored in any way," Ada said.

She was fueled by her anger, if not consumed by it. "I want his papers removed from the center."

"Everything we have was written by him or about him," Claire pointed out. "Legally the papers belong to Jonathan."

"Then give them back to him," Ada snapped.

"Of course," Harrison said. He opened the safe, took out the elephant hide briefcase, and handed it to Claire with his bare hands. "White gloves, Harrison," she wanted to say. "It's still an important document. Show some respect." But she took the briefcase in silence, walked down the hall to her office, laid it on her desk, and put on her own white gloves. She went to the tower, collected the rest of the archives, brought them back to her office, and began putting them in a box. The last item to enter the package was the elephant hide briefcase.

Legends rarely yielded to fact. Regardless of the reality of the person, the legend of Jonathan Vail could well continue. Years from now, a historian somewhere might present a paper attempting to establish that the person who was now in prison really had written *A Blue-Eyed Boy*. Whoever held the notebook at that point would be in possession of an extremely valuable document. Claire hated to relinquish the briefcase, but she knew she had to, so she dropped it in and sealed the box shut. She took off her gloves, noticing as she did that they had accumulated a fine layer of canyon dust. She put them in an envelope, wrote her name on it, the date, and her former position as archivist for Jonathan Vail. She sealed the envelope tight. On her lunch hour, she stopped at her bank and locked it in her safe deposit box.